Muddy

Meets

An Arach-A-Doo

Written by
Amanda Stone Norton

Cover and Interior Illustrations by
Veronica V. Jones

Interior Journal Illustrations by Amanda
Stone Norton and Veronica V. Jones

RISING PHOENIX PRESS

To Taylor
~Stay Curious!
Amanda Stone
Norton

Published by Progressive Rising Phoenix Press.
www.progressiverisingphoenix.com

Printed in the U.S.A.

ISBN: 978-1-940834-29-0   1940834295

"I think, at a child's birth, if a mother could ask a fairy godmother to endow it with the most useful gift, that gift should be curiosity."
- Eleanor Roosevelt

For mi Hija, Madeleine Stone. Stay curious.

Special thanks to my husband, Matt Norton, for encouraging me to "go for it;" my mom, Brenda Stone, who was never a fan of spiders, but always a fan of me; Ileana Valdez Villegas, for helping me keep it real; Beth Hall, my biggest cheerleader; and entomologist Gail Manning, for making sure my *bichos* had the right number of legs. *¡Muchas Gracias!*

Chapter One
A Scrumptiously Crunchy Scare

Inventing creative breakfast concoctions was a hobby of mine. While waiting for the water to boil in the microwave, I whisked a package of instant oatmeal with a couple of crushed Fig Newtons, half a chopped apple, a scoop of crunchy peanut butter, and a handful of Cheerios.

DING!

After pouring the hot water into the mixture, I grabbed my spoon and sat down at the kitchen table to eat. Dee-lish!

I took a break from inhaling my breakfast to look out the bay window, enjoying all the reds, yellows and browns that filled my yard. This time of year the leaves exploded with color.

That's when I saw her.

"*¡Hijole!*" I yelped, falling off my stool.

"Ouch," I groaned, rubbing my rear-end. "Girl, what's wrong with you?" Grabbing the top of the table, I pulled myself off the floor. "It's only a spider!" Normally, I would never, ever, let a spider scare me like that, but this was not a typical spider.

I walked over to the window to get a better look. The spider was spinning a web that spanned from the edge of our kitchen window to the corner of the roof over the back porch. Almost two feet wide and two feet tall, it was the biggest web I'd ever seen, which makes sense because it was made by the biggest spider I'd ever seen! The spider's black body, covered with yellow stripes, was the size of a quarter. Her yellow and black legs branched out like needles from her body.

"*Ven acá,* Mamá," I called out to my mom, who was in the hallway organizing files into her briefcase. "You've gotta see this wicked-looking spider."

"I'm coming, Muddy. Hold on a sec."

When I was born, my parents gave me a long name that's just luscious to say—Madeleine Mariella Milagros Morales. I'm named after Papá's French grandmother, his Italian great grandmother, Mamá's Mexican mother, and Papá's Costa Rican father. My family is one gigantic stir-fry of countries who obviously loves the letter M. But no one calls me by that name anymore—at least not after an incident last summer at Bill's Pond involving me, a lot of mud and a legendary swamp monster. Now

everyone calls me Muddy Madeleine or Muddy for short.

Mamá placed her coat and briefcase on the kitchen counter and walked toward the table. My dog, Murphy—another M name—bolted from behind her legs, flashing toward me like a streak of lightning. This 160-pound Saint Bernard jumped up, pounding his front paws onto my shoulders. He knocked me against the very window I had just leapt from moments ago and covered my face with slobbery kisses.

"*¡Buenos días*, Murphy!" I said, scratching behind his ears. Then I pushed him away and grabbed my napkin from the kitchen table to wipe his drool off my face.

Murphy sauntered to the porch door and whimpered. Mamá opened the door, and he charged into the backyard, chasing after some squirrels occupying his territory.

Mamá turned her attention to me. Giving me a hug, she asked, "*¿Dónde está tu araña?*"

"*¡Ahí está!*" I said, pointing to the corner of the window. "There's my spider."

"Oh, wow, *Hija*! You weren't kidding. She is wicked-looking."

We had a bit of time before I had to catch the bus

to school, so we stood at the window and watched the spider work. She walked along the web, pulling silk from her body with her two hind legs. Those long and lanky legs moved quickly as she connected each new strand of web to the next. She looked like she was playing an invisible violin. I had never seen a spider make a web before, and this was *muy* coolio.

"Looks like she's moving in," said Mamá. "Let's give her a name."

"What should we call her?"

"How about Charlotte? *Charlotte's Web* was my favorite book when I was your age."

"Nah! Every spider gets named Charlotte. Let's do something different ... uh ... how about Hilandera?"

"A Spanish spinner?"

"Yeah, 'cuz we found her spinnin' her web," I replied.

"I like it," said Mamá. "Very unique. Hilandera it is."

I wanted to stay and watch Hilandera work her web, but the bus was almost here and I still had to finish my breakfast. Returning to the kitchen table, I gobbled up the last few bites of my slightly soggy, but still scrumptiously delicious oatmeal.

After hugging Mamá, I grabbed my backpack. "*Adiós*, Hilandera," I yelled and ran out the front door.

Chapter Two
Spiders on the Brain

I've never been one to shy away from anything in the biological realm, whether it's an insect, amphibian or amoeba. Creepy crawlies are the coolest—spiders included, as is anything that requires me to get my hands dirty or my mind racing. And believe me, Hilandera had my mind moving as *rápido* as a cheetah chasing a gazelle.

Having never studied a spider before, this was my chance to get to know one up close and personal. I could not stop thinking about her. Had she finished her web? What would it look like? Did she catch anything to eat yet?

Hilandera had me so distracted that I totally messed up my solo in music class. Instead of singing, "She'll be comin' round the mountain when she comes," I belted out, "She'll be spinnin' round her web all day long." Everybody laughed—except Ms. Zozone, my music teacher, who raised her eyebrows and shook her head at my unexpected revision. *¡Qué verguenza!* I thought. I was so embarrassed.

Then, during our math lesson, Ms. Villegas caught me using my compass to create web-like designs around the angles she had assigned us to draw.

"Got spiders on the brain today, Muddy?" asked Ms. Villegas, looking over my shoulder.

"*Sí*, Ms. V. ... A big one."

Gregory, who had been my best *amigo* since our diaper days, leaned toward my desk. "What's that, Muddy?" he asked.

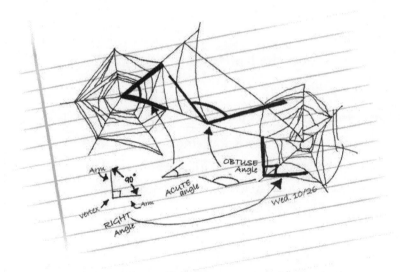

"Nothing really. I drew a web around my angles."

He turned his attention to Ms. Villegas. "Can I do that, too? Draw a picture with my angles?"

"Of course, Gregory," said Ms. Villegas, with a

smile. "Muddy, why don't you show the rest of the class your design?"

Feeling on top of the world, I jumped at the chance to share my work. After they saw my web, my classmates started drawing pictures of their favorite things—using angles here, there and everywhere.

Gregory ended up drawing a tent with twelve different angles. Another friend of mine, Javier, sketched his favorite climbing tree, highlighting the angles where the branches came together. Ava, my closest *amiga*, wants to design flying cars when she grows up. She showed off her hovercraft along with all the angles she used to draw it. My friends praised me with high fives and fist bumps for making math so artsy.

Even with all the attention, my mind was still stuck on Hilandera. I couldn't wait to get home and see her. I needed a new science project for the semester and she might be it.

* * *

The bus ride home from school felt as long as the school day. Normally, I liked hanging out with my friends on the bus—sharing the latest buzz, trying out new jokes and getting into spitball fights with the sixth graders—but today was different. I really wanted to get home.

As fifth graders, my friends and I sat toward the back of the bus between the fourth and sixth graders. I have no idea who created the seating chart or when it was first established—no one had ever told us where to sit or why we had to sit there—we just seemed to know. Kindergarten in the front and sixth grade in the back.

The chatter for the day was Halloween, which was coming up next week, and what costumes everyone would wear to school. I sat next to Gregory, who was turned around backwards in his seat talking to Javier behind us. They were trying to figure out matching outfits, tossing ideas back and forth. I heard something about bringing back the '80s and making 'big hair bands' cool again. That did it for me and I totally tuned out—'80's retro was not my thing. Anyway, I didn't have much to contribute to the conversation. Mamá and I had finished my costume weeks ago. I was going as Jane Goodall, wearing safari clothes with a dozen stuffed chimps pinned all over me.

"OUCH!" I yelled, grabbing my ear and looking around to see who had flicked it.

I saw Ava, sitting across the aisle, staring at me.

"*¿Qué pasa?* Why'd ya do that?" I asked, giving her a dirty look.

"You were totally ignoring me," she said. "What's with you today, *amiga*?"

"Um … well … I got this new science project going on at home, and—"

"You and your science projects," she teased, shaking her head. "To catch you up, we were talking about stopping by Ms. Carol's house and checking out all her 'dee-core.' Javier said he saw her hanging some skeletons this morning before school. Wanna come?"

Ms. Carol was obsessed with Halloween and her house was the scariest on the block. She didn't do anything halfway—creepy music, chainsaws and gallons upon gallons of fake blood. One year, she strapped her husband in a wooden chair and pretended to electrocute him, sparks and all. Every year we watched her build her spook-house, otherwise, we'd never have the guts to go up and ring the doorbell on Halloween night.

"Not today, gal," I said.

Ava let out a sarcastic huff. "Let me guess … science project?"

"Yep."

"Gonna tell me what it is?"

"Nope."

"You know I can't stand secrets."

"*Yo sé.*" I smiled. "I live to make you suffer."

She stuck her tongue out at me and then giggled.

When the bus stopped at my street, I hollered goodbye to the gang and pushed my way to the front.

I heard Gregory ask Ava where I was going in such a hurry.

"She's on another one of her science kicks," replied Ava. "We'll catch her tomorrow."

As soon as my feet hit the pavement I started running. Passing Ms. Carol's house, I noticed she had added some fake buzzards, covered in 'blood,' eating something that looked like a dead zombie. Even though I was tempted to stop, I kept running.

By the time I made it to my fence, I was panting. Murphy was waiting right there, ready to clobber me as soon as I walked through the gate. But I came prepared. Huffing and puffing, I took off my backpack, unzipped it and pulled out an apple I had saved from lunch. Red was his favorite, but green would have to do.

"Look what I got for ya, boy," I said, waving it near the fence, but still out of his reach. "A yummy *manzana.*"

"RAWF! RAWF!" he barked. Drool dripped from his mouth.

I chucked the apple as far as I could throw and he bounded away.

"What a fruit," I said and quickly grabbed my bag, opened the gate and ran to the front door, slamming it behind me.

"Whew!" I dropped my bag to the floor and dashed a few more steps to the kitchen window.

There she was, sprawled in the middle of her web. I couldn't believe it. The web was finished, and it looked even bigger than it did this morning. But I saw something strange. Hilandera's web had a zigzag that looked like a zipper running from the top, through the center and all the way down to the bottom of the web. What in the world was a zigzag doing there? Why did she do that? *¿Por qué?*

"Oh, yeah," I said to Hilandera, tapping on the glass. "You're definitely my new science project."

Chapter Three
Taking the Helm

On the bus ride to school the next day, I told Gregory about Hilandera and asked him if he'd ever seen a web with a zigzaggin' zipper.

"A zipper, Muddy? Really?" He chuckled. "So, what? Does it unzip into two pieces?"

"Don't be silly. It just looks like a zipper." I pulled my journal and pen out of my backpack and drew a picture of the web. While I sketched, Gregory finished his morning primping, pulling his long, black, corn-rolled hair into a pony tail.

Guess who woke up late today, I thought. My dark brown hair was cut into a short bob. A quick comb here and there, then add a headband and I'm ready for the day.

Drawing an accurate rendition of Hilandera's web on a bouncy bus turned out to be difficult. Just as I was about to finish my last zigzag, the bus hit a pothole, causing my zag to streak down, right off the page and onto my pants.

19

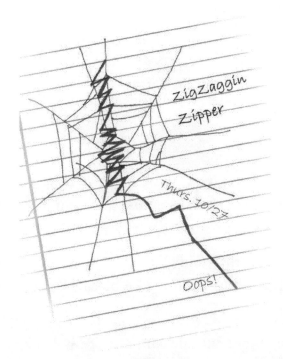

ZigZaggin Zipper

Thurs. 10/27

Oops!

Dang-it! I licked my finger and tried to rub the blue mark off my tan pants. Never worked before, but I had to try. What's that old saying—insanity is doing the same thing over and over again, but expecting a different outcome? Yeah, that's me. But I'm not insane. I'm a scientist.

Having failed to remove the stain, I returned my attention to my drawing. Even with the long tail, it was still a decent sketch of the real thing.

"That's cool," said Gregory, studying the picture.

Ava, who was sitting in front of us today, popped her head above the back of her seat. She reminded me of one of those Whac-A-Moles at Chuck-E-Cheese.

"What's cool?" she asked.

Gregory pointed to my drawing. "That is."

"Watcha drawing a zipper for, *amiga*? You giving up all that science mumbo-jumbo for fashion design?"

I pretended to laugh. "Ha! ... Ha! ... Ha!" And then, with my notebook, I whacked her on the head, like the mole she was. "You believe in all that mumbo-jumbo, too, and you know it!"

She stuck her tongue out at me and plopped back down in her seat.

"Told you it looked like a zipper," I said to Gregory.

"Yeah, yeah, yeah."

"So have you ever seen a web like this before?" I asked.

"Nope. Let's ask Ms. Villegas about it," he suggested.

I grinned. "You read my mind, pal."

* * *

21

While working on our individual lessons, I raised my hand and Ms. Villegas came over to my desk.

"*¡Hola*, Muddy*! ¿Qué pasa?*" she asked. "What's up?"

I told her about Hilandera and her wacky web, and Ms. Villegas said she would help me during recess to research some information.

Gregory's desk was to the left of mine. He leaned over, elbowed me in the ribs and whispered, way too loudly, "Hey Muddy, ask her if I can stay, too."

Ms. Villegas smiled. "*Sí*, Gregory. You can stay, *también*."

* * *

BRRRING! BRRING! BRRRING!

The recess bell rang, and everyone ran outside. Everyone, that is, except me and Gregory.

"Come over to the computer and let's learn about this spider," said Ms. Villegas.

We dragged our chairs from the second row to the front of the classroom.

Ms. Villegas pulled the chair out from under her desk and offered it to me. "Muddy, since we are researching your question, you get to sit at the helm."

She often shared 'the helm'—also known as her desk—with her students, but this was my first chance to sit there. Ms. Villegas dreamed of sailing the seven seas and often told us our classroom was like a ship, traveling around the world gathering knowledge.

"*¡Qué padre!*" I exclaimed and sat down in her chair. "Just call me *la capitana!*"

Gregory plopped into his own chair and sighed. "Lucky duck."

"C'mon, Gregory," I said. "Don't be upset. We're searching the Web for a web." I snorted, cracking up at my own joke. "Ha! Ha! Get it?"

He grumbled, shaking his head. "Yeah, I got it. But it's not funny enough to snort about, Muddy." Gregory never laughed at my jokes, but I know, deep down, he really liked them.

Ms. Villegas sat in my chair. "Type 'zigzag spider webs,' and let's see what we find," she suggested.

That's what I did and instantly a picture of a spider that looked just like Hilandera popped up on the screen. "*¡Esa es!*"

Gregory cringed. "That's her? ... Wow! ... She's a monster." He stared at her long lanky legs and yellow and black masked body. "I'm not sure I wanna help ya with this science project."

"*No tengas miedo*, Gregory," I teased. "Don't be a scaredy-cat."

"The spider may look frightening," said Ms. Villegas, "but it's not at all. I know this type of spider and have seen it in my garden at home. While she has venom glands she's perfectly harmless."

"Venom? *¿Qué es eso?*" I asked.

"It's poison delivered through either a bite or a sting," explained Ms. Villegas. "All spiders have venom, but not all spiders' venom is harmful to people."

"Wait a minute, Ms. V. You said it's not harmful to people, but what about dogs?" I asked, feeling worried.

She chuckled. "No need to worry about Murphy. This spider won't hurt dogs either, too much fur." Ms. Villegas had met Murphy last spring at Bill's Pond when he jumped up to give her one of his famous slobber kisses.

"Whew. That's good to know."

Ms. Villegas pointed to the computer screen. "This spider is a black and yellow *Argiope*."

"An our-guy-what?" I asked.

"Ar-GUY-oh-pee," she annunciated. She asked us to repeat it after her to make sure we pronounced it correctly.

25

After three tries we finally got it right. "Now that we know how to say it, what does it mean?" asked Gregory.

"It's the spider's scientific name. We talked about this last week in class—plants and animals have both scientific and common names," reminded Ms. Villegas. "*¿Te acuerdas?*"

"Oh *sí*," I said. "I remember. So what's Hilandera's common name? That's probably easier to say."

"Why don't you tell me," suggested Ms. Villegas, pointing again to the computer screen.

I scanned the webpage and found the answer. "It says that the ar-GUY-oh-pee is also known as an orb weaver spider."

"Well, that's not much help," complained Gregory.

"Actually, it is, Gregory," said Ms. Villegas. "The word 'orb' refers to something circular, and an orb weaver spider is a spider that spins a round, flat web."

"Oh." Gregory huffed. I could tell he didn't like being wrong.

"But that's its family name, not its common name," continued Ms. Villegas. "Spiders are grouped together into families by the type of web they make.

Take another look and tell me Hilandera's common name."

I scrolled down the page while Gregory leaned in to get a better view.

"There it is," he said, pointing to the screen. "Says right there that she's a garden spider."

"*Muy bien*," said Ms. Villegas.

Gregory smiled. "Now let's find out about that zigzaggin' zipper. Keep scrolling down, Muddy."

Ms. Villegas blocked the computer screen with her hand. "Just a minute. Before we find answers about the web, I want to know your hypotheses about the zigzag."

Gregory's lips curled up and his eyes narrowed. "What the heck is a hypo-THEE-sis?"

Chapter Four

The Zigzaggin' Zipper

Ms. Villegas laughed. "It's pronounced hy-POTH-ee-sis, Gregory."

"I know that word," I said confidently. "You mean our guesses."

"A hypothesis is more than a guess, Muddy. It's an educated guess." Ms. Villegas pointed to a picture of an orb-weaver's web on the monitor. "Take a look at this picture and tell me what you think based on what you see and what you already know."

I leaned back in my chair and considered her question. Why does she need the zigzagging zipper? My mind traveled back to the other day, when I walked through a web strung up between two trees at Bill's Pond. I never saw it. I could only feel it sticking to my face.

Gregory laughed.

"¿Qué?" I asked, snapping back into the present.

"Your tongue is sticking out, Muddy."

"You know my tongue always sticks out of my mouth when I'm thinking ... and like you should talk. Look at your pencil."

Gregory pulled his pencil out of his mouth. He had chewed the eraser clean off. "Alright," he said, punching me gently on my shoulder, "let's get back to hy-POTH-ee-SI-zin'."

He put what was left of his pencil back into his mouth, while I returned my tongue to its proper thinking place between my lips. Where was I? ... Oh, yeah, Bill's Pond.

"*¡Lo tengo!*" I announced excitedly. "I got it! The zigzag's a warning so people won't run into the web. Like a big stop sign that says '*¡Hola!* I'm right here.'"

Ms. Villegas smiled. "*Muy bien*, Muddy. *¿Qué te parece*, Gregory? What do you think?"

"Ya know," he said pulling the chewed-up pencil out of his mouth. "I was thinkin' that the zigzaggin' zipper could protect Hilandera."

"In what way?" asked Ms. Villegas.

"Most of her web is invisible, but she's so colorful with those yellow and black stripes. I think the zigzaggin' zipper helps hide her."

"Like camouflage?" asked Ms. Villegas.

"Yeah. ... Muddy's shirt made me think of it," he said, looking at my green and brown camo-designed shirt.

Ms. Villegas raised an eyebrow. "Do you think the zigzag could be both a warning signal and a hiding space?"

"*Sí*. Why not?" I said, pointing to the picture on the screen. "Look. The zigzag is thicker in the middle, and that's where she sits. I think the zigs and zags are thick enough to hide her—"

"And the zigzag," added Gregory, "thins out as it stretches to the top and bottom of the web. That could help others see it so they don't run into it."

"*¡Excelente!*" smiled Ms. Villegas, clapping her hands together. "*¿Tienes otras ideas?*

"I have another idea," I said. "Hilandera made it zig from the top and zag down to the bottom. Maybe it helps hold the web together. Kinda like the wood on the back of a kite." Papá had taken me kite flying last weekend and my dragon-flyer gave me the idea.

"Another great idea." Ms. Villegas pointed to the screen. "Scroll down a bit, Muddy. Let's see what the experts say."

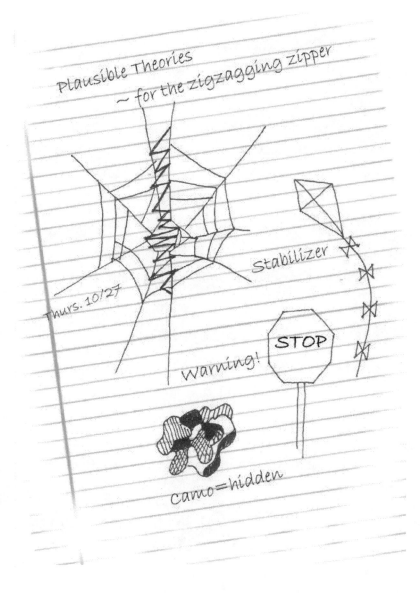

Plausible Theories
~ for the zigzagging zipper

Thurs. 10/27

Stabilizer

Warning!

STOP

camo=hidden

I did as she asked.

"Stop," she said, tapping on the screen. "It says here scientists use to think the zigzag stabilized the web and that's why they named it the stabilmentum. But they later discovered that research could not support that hypothesis."

"Oh." I sighed. "I was wrong."

"Not entirely," said Ms. Villegas. "You and Gregory had other hypotheses, too, and both those are listed here as plausible."

"Plausible?" I asked.

"That means possible" said Ms. Villegas.

"Oh, yeah," I said, shaking my head. "I knew that."

"The point," she encouraged, "is that you are coming up with the same ideas as the experts."

"Coolio!" I said, smiling at Gregory.

Ms. Villegas looked back at the screen. "Gregory, does it say anything else about the stabilmentum?"

"Here, Gregory," I said, getting up from the captain's chair. "You take a turn at the helm."

"Thanks, Muddy." Gregory beamed and we switched seats.

"Scientists also think," read Gregory, "the sta-bil-men-tum could be used to attract prey. The silk web reflects light, and the bigger the design the more light it reflects to attract insects."

"That means dinner!" I exclaimed.

"*Sí, asi es*," said Ms. Villegas, nodding her head. "That it does."

I sighed. "They have lots of theories about this zigzaggin' zipper—"

"And all of them sound plausible to me," interrupted Gregory.

"Nice vocab word, pal," I teased, dramatically rolling my eyes. "Who knows, but maybe all of the scientists' hypotheses are right."

"Don't make fun of me, vocab queen!" he returned my jab. "You just said—"

BRRRING! BRRRING! BRRRING!

"Saved by the bell." I giggled, patting him on the shoulder.

"That's the end of recess," said Ms. Villegas. She looked at Gregory. "My turn at the helm."

Gregory reluctantly gave up the captain's chair and pulled his back to his desk.

"Thanks for helping, Ms. V," I said.

"*De nada,* Muddy. Were all your questions answered?"

"*Sí y no.*"

"What do you mean?"

"Our Web research brought up more questions than I had before we started."

She laughed. "Learning tends to do that, Muddy."

"It sure does," I said and returned to my desk, dragging my chair behind me.

Not long after I settled back into my seat, Gregory nudged me in the ribs with his elbow. "What's wrong, Muddy? You look upset."

"Why ya say that?"

"Well, you've got this crinkle above your nose and your tongue's stickin' out again. What gives?"

I laughed and shook my head. "I'm not upset, pal. Just thinking about Hilandera's diet."

"What about it?"

"I'm wondering what she's gonna eat and when. I haven't seen anything in her web yet."

"How about I follow you home today and we check it out?"

35

"Coolio!" I said and we exchanged a fist bump.

Ava walked by, giving us a questioning look. "Where in the blazes have y'all been?"

Chapter Five
The Murphinator

Ava and Javier had soccer practice so Gregory was the only one to come to my house after school. We hung out for a bit in front of Ms. Carol's house to scope out her new spooks. I laughed when I noticed the newest addition to her front yard—a gigantic tarantula the size of a punch-bug Volkswagen.

Ms. Carol was a professional artist and her props looked like the real deal. She didn't miss a single detail, down to the spider's eight eyes and the long hairs on each of its eight legs.

Gregory stared at the realistic looking spider and turned a ghostly white.

"C'mon, pal," I said, patting him on the back. "Let's go see the real thing."

Just then, Ms. Carol walked out the front door, her arms filled with bulky plastic sheets. She waved and walked toward us. "I think a storm's on its way, kiddos. Before heading home, will you help me get this spider covered? I'd hate for her to be ruined before the big day."

I looked to the sky and saw clouds rolling toward us. "Oh, yeah. I'll help."

"Me, too," said Gregory.

Together, the three of us, using a combination of stakes and packing tape, secured the plastic tarps over and around the spider.

"Thanks, kiddos," said Ms. Carol. "I think we might have saved her." She smiled. "For helping me, I'll make sure you get a couple extra treats in your Halloween bag this year."

"Coolio," I said.

"Yeah, thanks," said Gregory, grinning from ear to ear.

Feeling the wind picking up, we ran the rest of the way home. As usual, Murphy was waiting in the front yard, jumping up and down like a Mexican jumping bean. The closer we came to the fence the higher the big boy jumped.

I laughed, wondering where he gets all that energy.

We stopped at the gate, refusing to enter until he calmed down. I learned this lesson the hard way when he rammed into me with such speed that I flew, rear-end first, into Mamá's garden, squashing her tomatoes and ruining my favorite pair of pants. Even though the garden was full of zucchini this time of year, I wasn't going to take any chances.

"Murphy, sit," I commanded.

"RAWF! ... RAWF!" he barked, with his paws still hanging on the fence.

"C'mon, boy. *Sientate*," I said with more authority. And down he went.

"Stay!" I held up my hand like a traffic cop signaling cars to stop, while Gregory pulled open the gate.

Murphy remained seated as we slowly walked through the entrance, that is, until he heard the click of the gate close behind us. Then he was off his haunches and coming straight for us, tail wagging and tongue flopping out the side of his mouth. Gregory quickly jumped behind a willow tree, but I wasn't so lucky.

"Uh, oh ... No! ... Stop! ... *¡Sientate!* ... Murphy, sit!" But it was too late. Murphy clobbered me. I crumbled to the ground, with him on top, covering me with sloppy kisses.

"What does he think he is?" asked Gregory, coming out from behind the tree. "A Chihuahua?"

"*¡Hola,* Murphy*!*" I giggled.

"I think The Murphinator gets bigger every day," said Gregory as he pulled Murphy's collar, trying to drag him off my lap. Gregory had nicknamed him 'The Murphinator' last summer for his role in the swamp monster affair at Bill's Pond.

"*Yo también te amo,* Murphy, but GET OFF!" I shouted. Using all the strength I could muster, I pushed him off me and quickly stood up. "I love you, but you gotta quit jumping on me like that."

Murphy quickly transferred his attention from me to Gregory and bounded over to give him a slobbery kiss.

"Yuck!" Gregory shoved The Murphinator away from him.

At this point, Mamá walked out the front door with her gardening tools in hand. "Murphy, come."

Murphy abandoned Gregory, ran to Mamá and sat down beside her.

"How do you do that, Dr. M?" Gregory asked, wiping slobber out of his hair with the sleeve of his jacket.

Mamá was the only person to whom Murphy listened. She wasn't a medical doctor, but a Doctor of Philosophy. When she got her PhD, her dad and *mi abuelo*, Pops, used to joke that she was officially licensed to Philosophize Higher and Deeper than anyone he knew.

"*¡Hola,* Gregory! The trick I use to train Murphy is this." Mamá pulled a dog biscuit out of her pocket and gave it to Murphy. "He likes treats."

I walked over to Mamá and gave her half a hug. She tussled my hair with her fingers.

"Quit it Mamá. You'll mess up my doo!" I said, backing away from her. "By the way, how's Hilandera? Did she catch anything to eat?"

"*No sé, Hija.* I just got home from work and want to finish up some gardening before the rain gets here. You'll need to check for yourself." She headed toward the vegetable garden in the back yard. "You kids have fun. Snacks are in the pantry." She looked at Murphy. "*Ven acá,* Murphy. You're with me."

He followed her to the garden, probably hoping to snag a squash or two.

Free of The Murphinator, we bolted up the stairs, through the front door, past the food-filled pantry, and straight to the kitchen window.

"There she is," I said pointing to Hilandera. "Isn't she *bella?*"

Gregory snarled his lips. "I wouldn't say she's

beautiful, Muddy. Ms. V may have said she was harmless, but your spider gives me the creeps. I mean, look at her! She has 'killer' written all over her."

"Yeah," I said, nodding my head. "I sure wouldn't want to be a bug trapped in her web, but there's something about her. With her long legs and those cool yellow strips, she's ... what's the word? ... *Elegante*."

Gregory rolled his eyes at me. "We'll just agree to disagree on that one." He turned his gaze toward the zigzaggin' zipper. "But she sure does make a cool-lookin' web."

"That she does, pal." I sat at the kitchen table and pulled my journal and pencil out of my backpack.

"Whatcha doing?" asked Gregory.

"I'm gonna draw her picture and write down the stuff we learned today before I forget."

"Okay. I'll go find us a snack," he said, and scampered to the pantry in search of something to munch.

While drawing her portrait, I thought I saw a moth in the upper corner of the web, but with further inspection I realized the moth was only a leaf.

"Hey, Gregory?"

"Yeah?" he hollered from inside the walk-in pantry.

"Do you know what spiders eat?"

"*Comen bichos*, Muddy," boomed Mamá's unexpected voice.

44

"*¡Ay, Mamá!*" I screamed and fell off my chair, hitting the floor with a thud. Murphy, who had followed her into the kitchen, ran over to me and worriedly licked my face. "You scared me to death."

Laughing, Mamá walked around the table toward me. "*Lo siento, Hija.* I thought you saw me. I'm sorry. Any blood or broken bones?" she asked, helping me off the floor and back into my seat.

"Nope, just a bruised ego." I patted Murphy's head and he sat down beside me. "*Oye,* Mamá. Did you just say that spiders eat insects?"

"*Sí, Hija.* They'll eat just about anything that gets trapped in the web." She looked around the room. "*¿Dónde está Gregory?*"

"Where do you think?" I teased.

She nodded with a smile. "Cookies are on the second shelf, Gregory. *Traete tres para nosotros, por favor.*"

Gregory poked his head out of the pantry. "What'd ya say, Dr. M?

I laughed. "She said to bring us three cookies, pal." Gregory had learned quite a bit of Spanish hanging out with me, but every once in a while we would surprise him with something new.

"You got it!" he said, emerging from the pantry

with a handful of cookies, definitely more than three. He headed toward the kitchen table to share his pilferings with me and Mamá. Murphy quickly ditched me for Gregory and his fistful of treats. What a traitor.

I grabbed one and took a bite. Dee-lish!

After gobbling down my snack, I returned my attention to Hilandera. I wanted to finish my drawing. "I hope she's able to catch some *bichos* in her web tonight. She's got to be hungry."

"Don't worry, *Hija*. I bet she'll catch something soon." Mamá turned to Gregory, who was stuffing his face with more of her cookies. She chuckled, shaking her head as she watched him devour a weekend's worth of baking. "Gregory, I came in to tell you that you need to head home. Dark clouds are moving in, and the weather forecaster is predicting a severe thunderstorm. I'm sure your mom wants you home in time for dinner."

"Can't he stay a bit longer?" I pleaded. Gregory stood beside me, nodding his head in agreement.

"Nope," she said. "If he stays any longer he'll get caught by the storm."

Gregory lived two houses down from ours, so he didn't have far to go.

"O-way," he mumbled as cookie crumbs fell from

46

his mouth. "Wee woo womorrow, Muwwy."

I snorted. "*¿Qué?*"

Gregory swallowed what remained in his mouth. "I said I'll see ya tomorrow." He laughed. "Thanks for the cookies Dr. M." Then he went to the window and tapped on the glass. "Hilandera, I know you're hungry, but don't ya go and eat my best friend tonight while she's sleepin'!"

KABOOM!

The thundercloud roared. Gregory quickened his pace, grabbed his backpack and ran out the door.

"Wadiós, wal!" I shouted, making fun of his cookie-accent.

Just as the door slammed behind him, the phone rang. The call was from Gregory's mom, telling him to come home—fast!

I looked out the kitchen window and the afternoon sky had quickly turned greenish-gray. Wind howled against the house, lightening lit up the sky and thunder rolled across the plains. In a brief flash of lightening I saw Hilandera clinging to her web with all her might as it blew wildly in the wind. The roof protected her from the rain, but the screen porch created a tunnel that pushed the wind directly into her web. The web bowed out like sails on a ship and Hilandera looked as if she was

47

hanging on for dear life. The sight made me think of
Ms. Villegas and her dream to sail the seven seas,
wondering if she could handle wind like this in the
middle of an ocean.

The storm continued through the evening. Every
time the thunder crashed, I rushed to the window to
check on my spider. She was hanging on, but barely.
Just before bed I visited the window one last time.
Mamá followed. Standing behind me, her fingers
tousled my hair.

"Hilandera is a tough spider, *Hija*. I'm sure she'll
be okay. C'mon, it's time for bed."

Reluctantly, I walked to my room. How will she
ever survive?

Chapter Six
Leave that Spider Alone

BUZZ, BUZZ, BUZZ screamed my alarm clock. I slammed my fist down onto the wretched machine to stop its horrible noise and rolled back over, pulling the covers above my head. Last night the storm was so loud I barely slept a wink. I was about to fall back asleep when one word popped into my head— Hilandera. Throwing off the covers, I sprung out of bed and hurried to the kitchen.

Oh please, please, please! I thought. Let her have made it!

Mamá and Papá were in the kitchen. Mamá sat at the kitchen table, drinking a cup of coffee, which she referred to as her nectar of life—whatever that means—and Papá had his head stuck in the fridge.

"*¡Buenos días, Hija!*" said Mamá. She smiled. "Guess who's still here."

"Yippee! She made it," I said, skipping to the window.

"Who made it, Muddy-gal?" asked Papá from inside the fridge.

"My spider."

"¿Araña?" Papá jumped, hitting his head on the top shelf of the fridge. "YOUCH!" he exclaimed, rubbing his noggin. "Where is it?" He grabbed the sports section off the table, rolled it up in his hand and swatted the paper through the air. "I'll kill that spider for you."

"Oh, no you won't, dear," giggled Mamá, taking the newspaper from his hand. "At least not this one. *Ven a la ventana y te presento,* Hilandera, Muddy's latest science project."

Papá joined me at the window. When he saw Hilandera he let out a long sigh. Quietly, as if talking to himself, he mumbled, "Why did it have to be a spider?"

My eyes widened and I stared at him in disbelief. "Are you scared of *arañas,* Papá?"

"Let's just say, they're not my favorite."

Mamá snorted at his comment and looked down at the coffee mug cradled in her hands, trying to hide the smile on her face.

Papá shot her a dirty look, which quickly turned to a grin. He put one of his arms around me. "All that matters is that you like her ... and ... that you never EVER bring her into this house. Promise?"

"Okay, Papá. *¡Prometo!*"

Mamá covered her mouth with one of her hands, trying to hold back a laugh.

Papá walked back to the fridge. As he passed Mamá he wagged his finger at her, which made the laugh explode through her fingers.

I turned my attention back to Hilandera.

She had survived, but her web was a wreck. The strands of silk reminded me of those faded flags attached to the top of car doors—the kinds that have flapped in the wind for so long the ends have unraveled. That's what most of Hilandera's web looked like, pieces of thread hanging from the roof. No more zigzaggin' zipper.

Dangling from one of the threads, she swung to another strand and connected the two. Her long and lanky legs moved, centimeter by centimeter, putting her into position to weave a new orbed web. She looked like she was dancing the two-step.

"I wonder where her silk comes from," I said, not expecting anyone to answer.

"From her spinerettes," replied Mamá.

Fixing her web
after the storm
Fri. 10/28

"Where are they?" I asked, smooshing my face against the window to get a better look.

"You can't see them from here, but they are on the bottom of her abdomen."

Mamá's comment surprised me. "I didn't know you knew so much about spiders."

"You inspired me, *Hija*," she said. "Like you, I did a little Web search yesterday day, too."

"Coolio!"

She looked at her watch. "Alright, time to get moving! Your bus will be here in *treinta minutos*."

Still looking at the window, I didn't move.

"*¡Ahora, Hija!*"

"Mamá, you know I don't need thirty minutes to get ready."

"Get dressed and put your school bag together. Then you can sit and watch Hilandera until it's time to leave," she replied. "I'll get your breakfast started."

I sighed and turned away from the window. "Okay."

"And here's your lunch, Muddy-gal," said Papá, placing my lunch box on the kitchen counter. "I'm off to work. Love you both."

Just as he said this, Murphy ran from the other room and jumped up to give him a kiss right on the smacker.

"*Yo también te amo*, Murphy" said Papá, taking the dog's gigantic paws off his shoulders and guiding them to the floor.

"Bye, Papá. Have a great day!"

Looking at me, he shook his head. "*¿Cómo se dice eso en Español*, Muddy-gal?"

While I knew Papá was only trying to help me practice my Spanish, I thought his pop quizzes were totally annoying! But I played along. "Okay ... *Adiós, Papá. Que tengas un buen día.*"

He nodded and smiled. "*Gracias*, Muddy-gal.

¡Excelente!" After giving Murphy's ears one more scratch he left for work, and I went to my room to get dressed.

I chose a purple shirt, a pair of striped pants that flared at the bottom and a matching quilted vest jacket. *Muy* coolio, I thought, looking in the mirror at my fashionable outfit.

The aroma of breakfast seeped into my room. I inhaled and smiled. Quickly, I ran a comb through my hair and stuffed my books into my school bag. There was no time to waste because Mamá was making my favorite breakfast of all time—*nopales con huevos*. Dee-lish!

I sat at the kitchen table, stuffing my face with cacti and eggs, and watched Hilandera work her web. Within a matter of minutes she had made tremendous progress. *¡Qué padre!* I thought. She moves fast.

"Alright, *Hija*," said Mamá, taking my plate. "Time to go."

"*Adiós*, Hilandera," I said, tapping on the window.

Mamá handed me my bag and hugged me goodbye. I headed off to school with a stuffed stomach, hoping Hilandera's would be full, too, by the end of the day.

Chapter Seven
Who Needs a *Bicho* Anyway?

BRRRING, BRRRING, BRRING rang the school bell.

"Buenos días, mis estudiantes," sang Ms. Villegas. "It's science time."

CLAP ... CLAP ... CLAP ... CLAP she began and we all joined in clapping our hands in four quarter time. This is how she started every science lesson— with a rap. She's so coolio!

Ms. Villegas vigorously clapped her hands and walked around the classroom, smiling at each student she passed. Then she began to chant.

Kingdoms of life
Oh, what a sight
Five diff 'rent kingdoms
To our delight

More kingdoms than that
Some experts say
But for the fifth grade
Five are plen-tay

Animals and Plants
Come to the ball
Without the others
The kingdoms would fall

Fungi, Bacteria
Then the Protists
Forget the last three
There will be some fits

The Animal Kingdom's
Our study today
We're rockin' out
With some inver-te-bray

We jumped to our feet, erupting in cheers.

Gregory nudged my ribs with his elbow. "She's really jammin' today. I think we inspired her yesterday."

"We sure did, pal."

Ms. Villegas took a bow and we returned to our seats. "Alright my young Einsteins," continued Ms. Villegas, slightly out of breath. "Based on the rap, what are we studying today?"

Gregory was the first to shout out. "Invertebrae!"

"*Sí*, invertebrates," nodded Ms. Villegas. "Those are members of the Animal Kingdom that do not have a backbone. And the invertebrates we're learning about today are insects."

57

A wave of murmuring engulfed the classroom.

Ms. Villegas smiled. "We're beginning our science lesson in a different way today by writing poems about our favorite insects."

"Not poetry," groaned Ava, sitting at the desk behind me. "Really, Ms. V?"

Ava couldn't stand anything that had to do with literature, and the only 'poetry' she liked was a good joke filled with potty humor. Farts, burps and poop made this blonde-haired, blue-eyed gal roar like a hyena, while poetry just gave her a headache. A few of my other classmates groaned as well, but not me. I love poetry. When I grow up I'm going to be a writer, and poetry is just another way to tell a story.

"I don't have a favorite *bicho*," blurted Chico. "A wasp stung me good this summer and, for that, *qué lleguen a la extinción* for all I care." He pretended to choke, wrapping his hands around his neck, letting his head fall to one side and making gurgling sounds.

¡Qué dramático! I thought. What a drama-king.

Many of my classmates whooped in support of Chico.

"Yeah, let them die."

58

"We don't need 'em!"

"*¡Qué Dios los bendiga,* bugs!"

"How many of you agree with Chico that insects should go extinct?" asked Ms. Villegas.

Everyone, except for Gregory, Javier and me, raised a hand.

"*¡Hijole!*" exclaimed Ms. Villegas. "So many of you don't like insects. That surprises me."

"Why, Ms. V?" asked Lihn, jumping up from her chair and turning around so everyone could see her. "Insects are gross." Scrunching up her face, Lihn looked like she was going to throw up. "BLAH!"

Everybody laughed, even Ms. Villegas.

And now make way for the drama-queen. Chico and Lihn liked to be the center of attention, often competing for the last word. Most of the time they argued, but today they appeared to be on the same side. This'll be *muy interesante,* I thought.

"Let's look at this issue in a different way," suggested Ms. Villegas as she sat on the helm, letting her legs dangle against the front of her desk. "How many of you like honey?"

Every hand shot into the air.

"Can you imagine a world without honey?" she asked.

"No way," exclaimed Chico. *"A mi me gusta la miel."* He smacked his lips. "I eat it every day on my almond butter sandwich."

Lihn chimed in. "And I eat honey on my pancakes in the morning. I love to draw flowers with my honey bear on each pancake before I eat it." She drew an imaginary flower in the air with her finger.

Wow, still agreeing? I thought. That's weird. Maybe these two are finally becoming friends.

"That sounds delicious and pretty," said Harper, our class cheerleader. She never has anything bad to say about anybody and loves to give out compliments.

"A mi me gusta la miel, también" said Ms. Villegas, "but we wouldn't have honey if insects didn't exist. Why do you think that is?"

"Bees!" exclaimed Gregory. "Bees make honey and bees are insects. If insects didn't exist, then honey wouldn't exist either."

"Muy bien, Gregory," encouraged Ms. Villegas.

"No bees means no *miel?"* questioned Chico. "Well, that just can't happen!"

"One-third of all the food we eat, Chico, is the result of pollination," shared Ms. Villegas. "And if pollinators are wiped out, then you'll lose more than your honey."

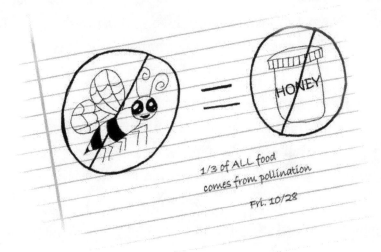

1/3 of ALL food comes from pollination

Fri. 10/28

"What else would go away?" asked Gregory.

With a more serious tone, Ms. Villegas replied, "No more apples, pears, grapes, *nopales*, lima beans, okra, and no more *aguacates* for guacamole—"

Everyone gasped.

"And that's just to name a few."

"Not *nopales*!" I exclaimed louder than I meant to, quickly covering my mouth with my hand. I couldn't imagine my life without *mi* mamá's mouth-watering *nopales con huevos*.

"Guacamole, too, Ms. V?" asked Javier from the back of the room.

"No avocados means no guacamole," responded Ms. Villegas.

I heard Javier huff his disappointment.

"Yeah, but it sure would be nice not to eat any more okra!" teased Ava. "Yuck!"

Some giggled at Ava's joke, but most of us just sat there in silence.

Harper broke the ice with a question. She raised her hand—the only one of us who always does. "I think I know, but I'm not sure. Can you please tell me what pollination means?"

Chapter Eight
Croakin' Bug-o-vores

"*¡Pregunta excelente*, Harper!" said Ms. Villegas, dropping her serious tone. "Excellent question. If you're to understand why insects are so important then you need to know about pollination."

She scooted off her desk and walked over to the board. "Lihn, since you like to draw flowers, please join me at the board and quickly draw a few. They don't have to be perfect."

Lihn skipped up to the whiteboard and drew five flowers all different colors. While she was drawing, Ms. Villegas showed off her own artwork by sketching a bee above the flowers.

Lihn hung out at the board after she finished.

"*Gracias*, Lihn." Ms. Villegas smiled, giving her a high-five. "You can sit down now."

"You're welcome, Ms. V."

"So here's what happens," started Ms. Villegas as Lihn skipped back to her seat. "Many plants produce pollen, which is necessary for the plants to reproduce—that means to have more plants." She put lots of orange dots in the center of Lihn's flowers where all the petals came together. "When the bee lands on the flower, looking for food or warmth, the pollen sticks to its body." She then drew orange dots on the bee. "The bee then flies to the next flower. When it lands, some of that pollen from the first flower falls off the bee onto the second flower. And *¡listo!*, you've got pollination."

Raising her hand again, Harper followed up with another question. "Are bees the only pollinators?"

Ms. Villegas shook her head. "I read yesterday that approximately 200,000 different species of animals are pollinators and only 1,000 of those are vertebrates—birds, bats and other small animals. The rest are invertebrates, like insects. So, let's do the math. How many different species of insects pollinate plants?" She went to the board and wrote 200,000 − 1,000. "Who's got the answer?"

"199,000!" hollered Ava.

Ms. Villegas gave a thumbs up. "*Muy Bien*, Ava."

"That's a lot of *bichos*," joked Chico.

Everybody laughed.

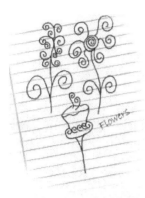

"And we need all those bugs, Chico," smiled Ms. Villegas, "because about 75% of all flowering plant species need pollinators to help them reproduce."

"What about the other 25%?" asked Lihn. "What helps them?"

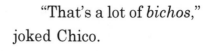

"I know that one!" exclaimed Ava. "Birds! They eat the seeds and poop them out."

I had to laugh. There she goes again with the poop.

"GROSS!" exclaimed half the class.

"COOL!" said the other half.

"You're right, Ava," laughed Ms. Villegas. "Animals do eat seeds, but we're talking about pollen. Seeds are the result of pollination. Without pollination there would be no seeds."

Ava grinned. "But y'all heard her. Seeds spread through poop."

I giggled and turned around to give *mi amiga* a fist bump.

"Seeds spread through a variety of ways, Ava," said Ms. Villegas. "Not just through feces." She paused for a moment, putting her hand to her chin in deep thought. "You know ... now that I think  about it, pollen and seeds spread in similar ways. They both travel with the help of animals, wind and water."

"So, if an animal ate a flower that had pollen on it and pooped it out—" began Chico.

"Then it could pollinate another flower!" interrupted Lihn.

Laughing, Ms. Villegas shook her head. *"No sé.* I don't know the answer to that one. I think we need a plant expert like a botanist, to help us with that. But, since we're on the subject of animals, how do you think they would be impacted if all insects went extinct?"

The class became quiet again. Twice in one day. That's a record.

"Does anyone have an idea?" asked Ms. Villegas. She looked around the room and her eyes stopped on me. "Muddy, you look like you might have a thought."

She must have seen my tongue sticking out.

"Well, I was thinking about Bill's Pond," I shared. *"Mi familia* and I spent *mucho* time there last summer and we saw tons of *ranas.* Mamá told me how the frogs lay low in the water or mud, waiting for a bug to fly by so they can snatch it up for dinner. ... So, I think frogs might croak if we didn't have insects." I snorted at my joke.

Gregory shook his head. Obviously, he didn't find it as funny as I did.

"I'm with Muddy," agreed Javier. "My lizards, Fred and Ted, only eat insects and they'd starve if insects didn't exist." Javier is obsessed with his lizards. He even named his band after them, the

Lizard Pickers. Yep, it's a band of banjo players.

Ms. Villegas nodded. "While not all lizards are like Fred and Ted, Javier, many would die out without insects. But those aren't the only animals that could become extinct. We could also lose anteaters, armadillos and some woodpeckers, too, just to name a few."

"No, not anteaters," exclaimed Lihn. "They're my favorite animals at the zoo."

"These animals are called insectivores," continued Ms. Villegas. "That means their diets consist mainly of insects."

"Sounds like a bug-o-vore to me," teased Lihn.

"Nice one!" laughed Chico.

I smiled. I knew those two would become friends sooner or later.

"And who would miss chasing butterflies in the

spring, listening to cicadas in the summer or catching fireflies at Bill's Pond on the Fourth of July?" asked Ms. Villegas.

Harper raised her hand. "All of those would go, too?"

"*Sí*," replied Ms. Villegas.

"I take it back," announced Chico. "I don't want *bichos* to go extinct."

"Me neither."

"No way!"

"*¡Me gustan los bichos!*"

I looked to Gregory and he was smiling. We were thinkin' the same thing—told ya so!

Chapter Nine
A Bug's a Bug

"Now that we've settled that and agree we need insects," said Ms. Villegas, "let's get back to our poetry."

Ava sighed. "Ah, not that again. I hoped you forgot."

"Nope. Not a chance, Ava." Ms. Villegas laughed, shaking her head. "I never forget an assignment. So, tell me. What insects do you plan to write about in your poems?"

"I bet I know what Muddy's gonna write about," shouted Gregory.

Everyone looked at me.

"Hush up, blabber mouth," I said between gritted teeth. After almost losing her in that storm, I wasn't ready to tell the rest of the class.

"Who are you going to write about, Muddy?" asked Harper.

Oh, well, I thought. The spider's out of the web.

"Sorry, Muddy," whispered Gregory.

I sighed. *"No pasa nada,* pal. Don't worry about it."

"Go ahead, Muddy," said Ms. Villegas. "Tell them about *tu araña.*"

So, I told them all about Hilandera, her zigzaggin' zipper web and how she barely survived the storm last night.

"She sounds awesome!" exclaimed Ava.

"I'd love to see her web, Muddy. Can I come over after school?" asked Javier.

Ms. Villegas interrupted the discussion. "Hilandera is an amazing spider, but she's not an insect."

"¿Qué?" I exclaimed, thoroughly confused.

"She is an arachnid."

"An arach-what?" asked Javier.

"What's the difference?" asked Lihn.

"Yeah. A bug's a bug," agreed Chico, earning a few giggles from our classmates.

"Does anyone know the difference between an arachnid and an insect?" inquired Ms. Villegas.

The room was silent. I looked around, not believing it had happened again. Three times in one day. It was no longer a record—it was a miracle.

Ava was the first to speak. "We don't even know what an arach-a-doo is."

Ms. Villegas laughed, as did half the class. She went to the board, erased Lihn's flowers and drew a three-column chart. At the top of the left column she wrote 'Arachnid.' In the right column she wrote the word 'Insect' and in the middle column she wrote 'Similar or Different.'

"Let's begin with legs," suggested Ms. Villegas. "How many legs does a spider have?"

"Hilandera *tiene ocho*," I announced. "Do all spiders have eight legs, Ms. V?"

"*Sí*, Muddy. All arachnids have four pairs of legs for a total of eight. Now, how many legs do insects have?"

Javier chimed in. "I feed Ted and Fred insects twice a day. Crickets, actually, and *tienen seis* legs. So, I say insects have six."

"Who agrees with Javier's statement that insects have six legs?" asked Ms. Villegas.

"They don't after I pull 'em off," kidded Chico, looking at me.

"Ha! ... Ha! ... Ha!" I'm not letting him anywhere near Hilandera.

"Not funny, Chico," said Harper, turning around in her chair and giving me a sympathetic look.

Chico smiled. "I'm just kiddin', Harper." He turned to me. "Don't worry, Muddy. I wouldn't hurt your spider."

Harper gave Chico a smile of approval, while I gave him a stare that said you better not!

"What do you think, my young Einsteins?" asked Ms. Villegas, returning us back to the subject. "Raise your hand if you think Javier is correct?"

Evidently no one wanted to second-guess Javier and our hands shot up.

"*¡Muy bien!* Insects have *seis* legs and arachnids have *ocho*," agreed Ms. Villegas, and she filled in the boxes on the board. "Now let's talk 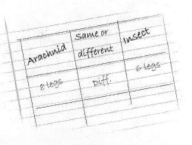 about their bodies. How many main body parts does an arachnid have and how many does an insect have?"

A rumbling mumble returned to the class. Ms. Villegas encouraged us to figure out answers in groups and she gave us time to discuss possibilities.

I kept to myself on this one, thinking about Hilandera and my observations of her. I pulled my notebook out from my desk, looked it over and raised my hand.

Chapter Ten

Come on in! Take off Your Skin! Rattle around in Your Bones!

Ms. Villegas gave me a nod. "*¿Sí*, Muddy?" Everyone got quiet again.

"I drew a picture of Hilandera yesterday and it looks like she only has a body and a head." I held up my picture so everyone could see, even turning around in my chair so those behind me could view my sketch.

"Muddy knows more about spiders than the rest of us," stated Gregory. "I agree with her. I think arachnids have two body parts."

"*¡Exacto!*" said Ms. Villegas. "They have an abdomen and a head. Thanks for sharing the picture, Muddy. You just demonstrated the importance of keeping a nature journal. *¡Muy bien!*"

Of course, I had a humongous smile on my face.

Ava tapped on my shoulder and I turned around. "Let me see that picture real quick, *amiga*."

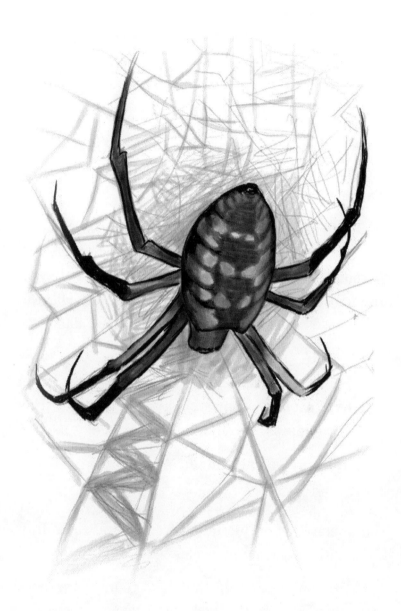

I gave her my notebook.

"According to this picture," proclaimed Ava, "Hilandera is just one big ol' bee-hind."

Trying to contain my laugh, I slapped my hand over my mouth. But I ended up making it worse—producing a loud snort, like a pig.

Ms. Villegas sighed. "Enough with the potty humor today, Ava. Now, give Muddy back her journal."

Ava passed it over my right shoulder, whispering in my ear, "That was a good one wasn't it, *amiga?*" Without looking behind me, I took the notebook, dropped it in my lap and gave her an over-the-shoulder fist bump, trying to make it look like I was scratching my back.

Ms. Villegas turned her attention back to the rest of the class. "Now, how about insects? How many body parts do they have?"

Harper raised her hand.

"*Sí*, Harper."

"When I draw pictures of ants, I always draw them with three round circles."

"Are you suggesting that insects have *tres* body parts then, Harper?" asked Ms. Villegas.

"Yes, ma'am. I am."

"You are correct," said Ms. Villegas.

Harper showed off her smile.

"Insects have three main body parts," explained Ms. Villegas, "and they are the head, thorax and abdomen." To the right of the grid, she drew a picture of the three body parts and labeled them. She then wrote '2 body parts' under the arachnid column, '3 body parts' under the insect column and the word 'Different' in the middle.

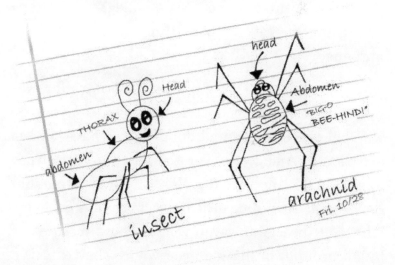

She continued. "Next, let's tackle the question about whether or not arachnids have antennae and wings. We haven't heard from you for a while, Lihn. What do you think?"

Lihn thought about the question and then shared a story. "We have tons of insects and arachnids at our house. They crawl everywhere, up and down the walls, across the floor and even in our cabinets. It drives my dad crazy. Mom says it's because we live so close to Bill's Pond. She told me that they love hanging out in the tall grasses around the edge of the pond, too. And when I walk through the grass, that's when I get the most chiggers and ticks. And you know, those bites make me scratch something awful. Mom likes to use Calamine lotion to help—"

"Lihn," interrupted Ms. Villegas. "Weren't you going to tell us something about wings or antennae?"

"Oh, yeah, that's right," giggled Lihn. She was notorious for getting lost in her own stories. "So with all the bugs around our house, I have tons of experience. And I've never seen a spider fly. They like to dangle, making it look like they're flying, but they're not. Scares me to death because they get in my hair. But insects are even worse. Those mosquitoes fly all around, biting me everywhere they can. I've been bitten on my ears, legs, neck, arms, and feet. Talk about itching! Now, that's when I really need some Calamine—"

"Back to the wings, *por favor*," reminded Ms. Villegas, her smile looking frazzled.

"Oh, yeah," said Lihn, finally getting to her point. "Insects have wings and arachnids don't. And thank goodness they don't. Can you imagine what it would be like to have spiders flying all—"

"I don't think all insects have wings," interrupted Gregory.

"*¿Por qué no*, Gregory?" asked Ms. Villegas.

"There's a giant ant hill in my back yard," he said, "and only a few of the ants have wings. But I do agree with Lihn that spiders don't have wings 'cuz I've never seen one either."

"Can you sum that up for us, Gregory?" asked Ms. Villegas.

"Yep," he said. "I hy-POTH-ee-size that arachnids don't have wings and some insects do."

"Nice vocab word, pal," I teased, elbowing him in the ribs.

"*¡Muy bien*, Gregory!" said Ms. Villegas, and she added those traits to the chart on the board. "Now for the antennae. What about those?"

"Based on my picture," I said, "Hilandera doesn't have any antennae so I hypothesize that spiders do not have antennae, but—"

"Copycat," jabbed Gregory, under his breath.

"... I don't have a clue about insects," I said and then stuck my tongue out at him.

"Butterflies do," said Harper, stretching her hand toward the ceiling. "My dad and I raised Monarch butterflies last year in a kit my grandma gave me for my birthday. All of them had antennae."

"Crickets do, too," chimed in Javier.

"Let's do this systematically," suggested Ms. V. "Does everyone agree with Muddy that arachnids do not have antennae?"

"Yes," everyone yelled together.

"And how about insects?" she asked. "Do all or only some of them have antennae?"

Not having enough information to answer the question, we started mumbling again.

"Alright," she laughed. "I'll give this one to you. All insects have antennae." And with that she wrote the traits on the chart, once again showing how arachnids and insects are different.

Ms. Villegas turned around and faced the class. "Now that we know some of their differences, let's learn about some of their similarities."

Ava leaned over my shoulder and whispered in my ear. "This is great, *amiga*. Thanks to you and your arach-a-doo she's totally forgotten about the poetry."

I laughed and Ava leaned back in her chair.

Ms. Villegas gave us a questioning look, like she knew we were up to something, but then continued. "Both arachnids and insects have more than one pair of eyes and both have exoskeletons."

"Ex-o-what?" asked Javier.

"Exoskeletons," repeated Ms. Villegas. "Whereas a human's skeleton is inside the body, an arachnid's or insect's skeleton is on the outside of the body. That's why it is called an EXO-skeleton. Exo, in Latin, means outside."

"So, Ms. V," inquired Ava, with a grin, "are you sayin' that insects and arach-a-doos are just a bunch of skeletons walking around?"

"Come on in! Take off your skin! Rattle around in your bones!" chanted Chico.

Everybody laughed.

"Not quite, Ava," smiled Ms. Villegas. "Their skeletons are in a different place than ours."

"It's like the armor a knight wears," I suggested, thinking about my favorite restaurant where the waiters wear medieval clothes and knights battle on horseback during the meal. "It protects them better—especially since they are so small."

"Nice analogy, Muddy," said Ms. Villegas. She turned to face the board and wrote the similarities in the columns.

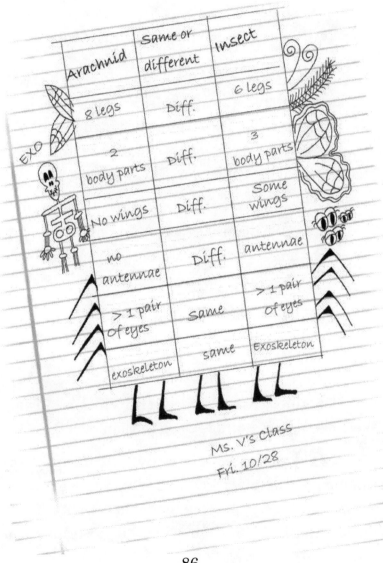

Arachnid	Same or different	Insect
8 legs	Diff.	6 legs
2 body parts	Diff.	3 body parts
No wings	Diff.	Some wings
no antennae	Diff.	antennae
> 1 pair of eyes	Same	> 1 pair of eyes
exoskeleton	Same	Exoskeleton

Ms. V's class
Fri. 10/28

"Ms. V?" asked Lihn.

"¿Sí?" said Ms. V, continuing to write on the board.

"You said they both have more than one pair of eyes. Why is that?"

Chico jumped in, "Why the better to see you with my dear." He snarled.

Ms. Villegas turned to face the class. "That's not too far from the truth, Chico." She laughed. "Researchers believe the front pair of eyes is used for seeing details, whereas, the other pairs watch for prey."

"How do you know so much about arachnids and insects, Ms. V?" I asked.

She smiled. "Because my parents are entomologists."

"What's that?" asked Lihn.

"An entomologist is someone who studies insects and arachnids." Ms. Villegas then pointed to the chart. "So, the next time you see an insect or an arachnid, will you be able to know which is which?"

"Yes, ma'am," shouted Javier. The rest of us nodded vigorously in agreement.

"Okay, then," she said. "Let's start writing our po—"

BRRRING! BRRING! BRRING!

Ms. Villegas looked at the clock on the wall and shook her head. "Well, I guess that's it for today."

"Yippee!" exclaimed Ava, jumping out of her chair. She began to chant and do some crazy-lookin' dance next to her desk. "No po-e-try to-day-hey! We got away to-day-hey!"

"I don't think so, *amiga*," I said, watching Ms. Villegas walk to the door, holding a stack of papers.

"I've got your poetry assignments right here," announced Ms. Villegas. "Make sure you get one before you leave because it's due first thing Monday morning."

Ava had been so busy dancing and chanting I was sure she hadn't heard the announcement— especially because she was still smiling.

I packed my bag and got in line to say *adiós* to Ms. Villegas.

When it was my turn to say goodbye, she handed me a piece of paper. "*Tener un gran fin de semana,* Muddy."

"I hope you have a great weekend too, Ms. V," I replied.

"Even though the assignment says insect, you're welcome to write about your arachnid instead."

"*¡Gracias*, Ms. V.!" I said and walked into the hallway. She's so cool.

"And here's your assignment, Ava," smiled Ms. Villegas. "Have a great weekend."

Ava looked at the top of the paper and read aloud, "Poetry Assignment: An Insect for Me. ... Ughh!" Her mouth gaped open in disgust. She looked up at Ms. Villegas, her eyes pleading for mercy.

"I told you, Ava," teased Ms. Villegas. "I never forget an assignment."

Chapter Eleven
The Lizard King

"Penny for your thoughts?" asked Gregory on the bus ride home from school.

"*¿Qué?*" I asked.

"Dunno what it means, but Grandma says it to me when I'm quiet. What gives?"

"I've been thinking about our poetry assignment and what I'm gonna write about."

"Hilandera, of course," he said in a know-it-all tone.

I rolled my eyes. "No, duh! But what should I write about her?"

"You got tons of choices. Her creepy legs, scary bee-hind—"

"It's called an ab-do-men," I corrected.

"That's what I said. Her scary ab-do-men," Gregory replied sarcastically. "Or how about how she survived that storm last night? You could get all touchy-feely with that."

I snorted. "You sound like you love poetry as much as Ava."

"Yo, *amiga*," hollered Ava, who was sitting with Harper two seats behind us. "Did I hear my name?"

I turned around and sat on my knees. "You know it! Just talking about how much you love poetry."

Ava pointed her finger into her open mouth, pretending to gag. "I was thinking about that, too. How about you and Gregory come to my house later today? I need an insect to write about and you two are the buggiest people I know."

Javier sat alone in the seat behind us, in front of Ava. He turned around and looked at her. "What about me? Can I hang out, too? I'm good with insects. Just call me cricket-man," he said, laughing at his own joke.

"Nah," teased Ava, shaking her head. "With all that banjo pickin' you do, you're the Lizard King."

"The Lizard King?" pondered Javier. "Yeah, I like it. Sounds cool!"

"Good," exclaimed Ava. "How about it, Muddy? Gregory? Harper? Y'all comin' over or what?"

"I'm in," said Gregory.

"Can't, Ava," said Harper. "Piano lesson today. Gotta practice for the big recital this weekend."

I hesitated to respond.

"You got something better to do, *amiga?*" questioned Ava.

"Well ... actually ... I do. Hilandera had a rough night and I want to check on how she's doing. This morning she was dangling on a string."

Ava pressed her lips together, breathing deeply out her nose. "Change of plans," she announced. "We're going to Muddy's. Then we can hit Bill's Pond after we check on that arach-a-doo of hers."

"Thanks," I said, smiling at Ava.

"Works for me," said Gregory. "Mom said I could hang out at Muddy's today, anyway. So I can go straight there."

"What about me?" insisted Javier.

"It's not an official party without the Lizard King," I giggled.

Javier gave his best attempt to look cool by sliding on his sunglasses, staring absently out the window and sticking his chin up in the air.

Gregory and I both laughed, but Ava didn't buy it. "Just be at Muddy's house in twenty minutes, cricket-man."

"Aghhhh!" sighed Javier, sliding off his shades.

The bus stopped at our road and Gregory sprinted to the front. "First one to Muddy's gets to squash a spider."

"Not funny!" I yelled out the cracked window.

While I hollered at Gregory, Javier jumped my turn in line to get off the bus. In his haste, he tripped, dropping his backpack, lunch box, coat and whatever else he was lugging home from school. His stuff was scattered everywhere, and I was stuck behind him.

"Sorry, Muddy," Javier mumbled. He was on his knees, reaching under a seat to retrieve his lunch box.

Watching Gregory sprint toward my house, I gave Javier a gentle shove. "Get movin' Javi. He'll eat all the cookies!"

"Cookies? Say no more." He grabbed the rest of his things and we shuffled to the front. Ava had to go home first, so she didn't get off with us at our stop. As the bus pulled away, she yelled out the window, "Be there in twenty, Muddy. And save me some cookies, Lizard King!"

Chapter Twelve
That's One Giant Arach-A-Doo

I was one step behind Javier as we chased after Gregory. We ran as fast as we could, knowing it was too late to catch him, but we had to try. I didn't think he'd really squash Hilandera, but I wasn't taking any chances.

Javier and I got to my house just in time to see Gregory pinned down on the ground by Murphy, who was giving him a slobber-bath.

"Stop ... no ... Murphinator, please. I give up," howled Gregory trying to push The Murphinator off his chest.

"That's what you get for threatening my spider, pal," I laughed.

As soon as Murphy heard my voice, he abandoned his wash duties and bounded toward me. While Javier gave Gregory a hand getting up, I distracted Murphy with a bear hug.

"Dang, Gregory," said Javier, wiping excess drool off his hand onto his jeans. "You are covered in dog-goo."

"Yeah," scowled Gregory. "He slimed me."

"I got a towel inside, pal. C'mon guys. Let's go see Hilandera."

Seeing Murphy's favorite ball nestled in the leaves, I picked it up and tossed it to the other side of the yard. As he pursued the bouncing bobble, we made our escape through the front door, slamming it behind us.

"*¿Muddy-gal, eres tu?*" yelled Papá from the study.

"*Sí*, Papá, It's me. Gregory and Javier are here, too, and Ava's on her way. *¿Te parece bien, Papá?*" I asked, poking my head into his study while the gang headed to the kitchen. I hoped he wouldn't mind I brought my friends home with me.

Papá looked up from his computer and gave me a smile. "*Está bien conmigo.* I'll be in here finishing up some work, so you kids have fun. I think we still have a few of Mamá's cookies in the pantry."

"If Gregory hasn't eaten them all by now."

"You better get going then," he said, giving me a wink.

I headed to the kitchen where I found Gregory already raiding the pantry and Javier standing by the window looking at Hilandera.

97

"You weren't kidding, Muddy," he said. "She's awesome! And that web—"

"Is she still working on it?" I inquired, not yet close enough to get a good view for myself.

"Looks done to me."

"*No es posible.*" I rushed to the window. Standing beside Javier, I saw it was, indeed, possible. Hilandera had completely repaired her web, zigzaggin' zipper and all.

"She did all that in just a few hours?" I wondered aloud.

"That's the coolest web I've ever seen," announced Javier. "What kind of spider is she?"

"An *Argiope*," I said.

"Okay, whatever," he snickered.

I laughed. "It's easier to call her a garden spider. ... Do ya see anything in her web that looks like food?"

"I got your food right here," said Gregory, carrying the cookie jar in his hands and a bag of chips wedged between his right arm and his side.

"Ha! ... Ha! ... Ha!" I said flippantly. "I'm being serious. After all that work she did today, she's got to be hungry."

"Sorry, Muddy. Wanna cookie?" he asked, sitting down at the table.

I smiled. "Yeah, in a minute, pal."

"I don't see anything on the web, Muddy. Other than the spider, it's empty." Javier turned to Gregory and held his hands slightly apart in front of his chest like he was catching a football. "Toss me one of those, Greg."

Gregory launched a cookie into the air, over the table and right into Javier's hands.

After taking a look out the window, I flopped down on a kitchen chair. "I didn't see anything either."

"How often do they eat anyway?" asked Gregory, ripping open the chip bag.

"Not a clue," I said. "Pass those over here when you're done."

He took a handful of chips out of the bag and pushed it across the table to me. I popped one into my mouth. Oh ... love me some sour cream and onion.

"Why don't we look it up?" suggested Javier. "Ya know, while we're waiting on Ava to get—"

"The wait is over, *amigos*." Ava burst through the doorway, "Fun has finally arrived."

"*¡Hijole!*" I blurted, spitting pieces of chewed-up chips out of my mouth onto the table. Why do people keep scaring me in my own kitchen?

Gregory and Javier roared with laughter.

Ava looked at the slobbery chips on the table and shook her head. "And people say I'm gross. Girl, that's disgusting."

I chuckled and she handed me a paper towel from the counter. While I wiped up my mess, Gregory caught Ava up on all she missed.

"So we're gonna figure out how long she can go without food, then head to the pond?" asked Ava.

"That's the plan," confirmed Javier.

"Groovy." Ava looked around the kitchen. "Now, will somebody please show me the spider that's causing all this fuss?"

I looked at Gregory and Javier. "Hey, guys. Will you introduce Ava to Hilandera while I ask my dad if we can use the computer?"

"Sure thing, Muddy," replied Gregory.

I left the kitchen and headed to the study, where I found Papá still sitting at his desk. He was holding a notepad in his left hand while typing with his right—hunting and pecking at the keyboard. "*¡Hola, Papá!* Can I use Mamá's *computadora* for a bit? We wanna do some research on Hilandera."

"*Claro que sí,* Muddy-gal," agreed Papá. "Let me know what you find out."

All the way from the kitchen, I heard Ava yell, "HOLY GUACAMOLE! That's one giant arach-a-doo!"

Papá laughed. "I think Ava just met your science project."

Chapter Thirteen
He or She?

Ava, Gregory and Javier had already moved some extra chairs over to Mamá's computer desk and sat there waiting for me, passing the potato chip bag among them.

"We're good to go with the computer," I announced.

"Are you sure we need to do this, Muddy?" asked Ava, wiping her greasy hand onto Javier's shirt. "She must've already eaten 'cuz she's humongous."

"I dunno," I said, "but I haven't seen any signs of leftovers."

"Yeah," agreed Gregory. "Don't they need to wrap up the insects into some kind of cocoon and let them marinate or something?"

I chuckled. "Like I said earlier, pal, not a clue."

"Alright then," agreed, Ava. "Let's do this and then get outta here. I gotta find me a bug to write about."

I smiled and sat in the chair directly in front of the laptop. "You got it, girl. How should we begin?"

"Try typing 'How often do arach-a-doos eat,'" suggested Ava.

"Oh ... wait a sec." I looked around the chair for my book bag. "Gregory, will you take the helm 'cuz I need to find my journal. We gotta write down what we find." I jumped up and ran to the hallway where I had dropped my bag. When I returned, pen and paper in hand, Gregory had already pulled up a website.

"We found something, Muddy," declared Javier. "It says here that ar-GUY-o-pees are carnivorous, so they only eat meat."

"Yeah," I said, sitting in Gregory's former chair. "That's what Mamá said. They eat *bichos*."

"Well, it says here," said Gregory, pointing to the screen, "they can also eat small vertebrates like geckos."

"No way!" hollered Javier. "That thing out your window can eat a lizard?"

"Better watch out Lizard King," joked Ava.

Javier shot her a nasty look to which she responded with a flirtatious wink.

"Only little ones," said Gregory. "I think Ted and Fred are safe."

Javier sighed. "That's a relief."

"Let's focus, y'all," scolded Ava. "Daylight's a wastin'."

"Okay, okay," I said. "Does it say anything about how often she eats?"

"How do ya know it's a she, Muddy?" asked Javier.

"Um ... I dunno," I said, looking toward the window. "I just assumed she was a she." *¡Qué verguenza!* I thought. What kind of scientist am I? How embarrassing.

"It says here," read Gregory, "females build bigger webs and are more visible than the males and—"

"Yeah, that arach-a-doo is visible alright" interrupted Ava. "But we don't have another web to compare it to. And, how big is big anyway?"

"If you'd let me finish," said Gregory, "then I'd tell ya."

Ava stood up from her chair and gracefully moved her arm in front of her. "Well then, please continue." She walked to the kitchen table and pulled a cookie from the jar.

Gregory continued reading. "... and that while the female is as large as 1.1 inches, the male is only .35 inches."

Girl = 1.1"
Boy = .35"
Fri. 10/28

"We need a ruler!" suggested Javier.

"Scoot back," I said to Gregory, which he did. I pulled open the middle drawer on the desk and grabbed the ruler. Handing it to Javier, I said, "Go see if you can figure out how big she is."

"How ya gonna do that?" asked Ava, leaning against the kitchen counter. "You can't get a good measurement through a window."

Gregory's eyes widened with curiosity. Looking at Javier, he asked, "Are you gonna touch it?"

"Sure, why not?" he responded, heading toward the back door.

"Oh, no you're not," I scolded. "You might mess up her web again, and think how awful it would be if a giant, seven million times your size, lifted you out of your bed!"

Javier responded sarcastically. "Well, then how are we gonna measure it if you won't let us touch it?"

Papá walked into the kitchen, "Touch what, Muddy-gal?"

I jumped up from my chair and ran to him. "You're tall enough, Papá. You can help us."

"*¿Ayudarte con qué?*" he asked.

I told him what we needed and his mocha skin turned *blanco*.

Taking his hand, I said, "All you gotta do, Papá, is hold the ruler close to her. No touching."

He looked squeamish and gave a nervous chuckle. "Don't worry, Muddy-gal. I have no intention of touching that spider." He squeezed my hand and then let go. Reaching out to Javier, he said, "I'll take that ruler."

Ava hollered, "Mr. M saves the day!" and the boys raised their fists into the air, shouting, "Whoop! Whoop!"

Papá smiled and walked toward the door. I could

tell he was trying to look brave in front of my friends, holding his shoulders back and his head high. But the smile on his face was all a show. The crinkle between his eyes and the shaking ruler in his hand said it all. Papá was terrified.

"I'm going with him," I announced to my friends who had already piled up beside the window to watch.

We walked outside together. I was surprised Murphy hadn't attacked us yet. He must still be in the front yard chewing on that old, gross ball, I thought.

Taking Papá's hand in mine, I said, "*Te prometo, Papá. Ella no es peligrosa.*"

He nodded. "I know she's not dangerous."

"*No pasa nada,* Papá," I encouraged.

Papá looked up at Hilandera and let out a deep sigh. "*Yo sé.* You're right. I'll be fine." He then turned his head toward the window. Seeing my *amigos* with their noses smooshed against the window, Papá snapped his head toward me and, with a sparkle in his eyes, said, "*¿Quieres hacer esto?*"

"Really? You want me to do it?"

"You bet. I'll lift you up and you can take the measurement."

"Coolio!"

107

He handed me the ruler and then lifted me over his head, settling me down on his shoulders. My legs rested on his chest. Slowly, I stretched my hand with the ruler toward Hilandera, careful not to touch her, and got the measurement—one inch wide.

Papá backed away from the web and helped me to the ground. I ran inside screaming, "She's a girl! She's a girl!"

He followed me into the kitchen, his shoulders looking much more relaxed, and grabbed a cookie from the jar. "Okay. *No más arañas para mí.* I'm heading back to the study."

"Thanks, Mr. M," said Gregory. "Couldn't have done it without ya."

Papá smiled and went back to work.

I needed to get us back on track. "Now that we know she's a she, let's figure out how much she eats," I said.

Javier jumped into the captain's chair and continued our Web search. We walked over to the desk and sat beside him. After reviewing four different sites, we still hadn't found anything.

Ava started getting anxious. She paced around the kitchen for a bit. Then she stood behind us, with her arms folded, tapping her foot impatiently. Eventually she walked to the counter, picked up one of Mamá's books and thumbed through it—

rather loudly. Our time was running out. Ava was an outdoorsy gal and being cooped up inside on a beautiful day was pure torture for her.

Leaning back in his chair, Javier sighed. "All I've found is one comment, two web pages ago, that said ..." he looked down at the notes he had written in my journal and read, "... no one is certain of how much a spider eats."

"Look here." Gregory pointed to the screen and read, "Every night the yellow and black garden spider consumes its web and then rebuilds it the next day."

"Seriously?" I asked.

"Yep," nodded Gregory, who continued to read. "The spider recycles the chemicals used in the web to make more silk. When eating the web, it also eats tiny insects stuck to the web."

"*¡Hijole!* I totally didn't expect that," I said, shaking my head in disbelief. "Guess I've been worried about nothin'."

Javier recorded the new information in my journal, while I grabbed some water bottles from the fridge.

"Let's get out of here," I suggested, handing one bottle to each friend. "We still have time to explore the pond."

When I tried to give Ava her bottle, she didn't take it. She was nose-deep into the book she had found on the counter.

"Hey, you guys," she said, still looking at the book. "I found something." She showed us the tattered cover of *Charlotte's Web* by E.B. White.

Remembering how nostalgic Mamá had become when we first found Hilandera, I thought she must have brought it out of storage to re-read.

Ava summarized for us. "Okay, so this spider is telling a pig how she eats a fly. When the fly lands on the web, the spider, named Charlotte—"

"We all know who Charlotte is," interrupted Gregory.

"I don't," said Javier. "Keep going, Ava, What's it say?"

Ava rolled her eyes at Gregory, smiled at Javier and continued her tale. "As I was saying ... Charlotte jumps on this fly, wraps it up in silk and then bites it." She scanned the page. "Yadda, yadda, yadda ... and now to the good part where Charlotte describes what she does to the fly." She read from the book, "'Delicious. Of course, I don't really eat them. I drink them—drink their blood.'"

Slamming the book closed, Ava looked at us with her eyes wide-open and her mouth in a grin.

"Hilandera is a blood-sucker!"

We stood there, staring at her in silence.

"Isn't that cool?" she asked.

Gregory was the first to speak, his upper lip curled in disgust. "Only you would find that cool, Ava."

I walked over to Ava. Putting my arm around her shoulders, I looked at the two boys. "I totally agree with you, gal. That's awesome!"

Ava turned to me and smiled. "I knew you'd think so, too, *amiga*."

"Let's add that bit of info to the journal," I suggested. Gregory handed me the notebook and I wrote 'blood sucker.'

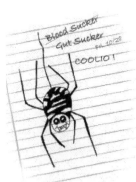

Meanwhile, Javier returned to the computer and quickly announced that he'd found something new. "I got more info on our blood-sucker," he said. We walked back over to the computer. "Says here that Hilandera has fangs, but she doesn't have any teeth. So to eat, she's got to suck up the fly." Javier read to himself for a second while we looked over his shoulders. He shook his head in disagreement.

"Yeah, I don't think it's blood, Ava. This website says the spider's venom liquefies the prey so the spider can drink the whole thing."

"That's even more coolio!" I exclaimed, writing down Javier's new information.

Gregory pretended to throw up. "Ugghh!"

"I really like this arach-a-doo," smiled Ava, patting Javier on the shoulder. "Nice job, Lizard King. Now let's get out of here 'cuz—"

"We know," teased Gregory. "Daylight's a wastin'."

I turned off the computer and we headed to the pond in search of an inspirational bug for Ava.

Chapter Fourteen

A Dash of Shakespeare with a Pinch of Curie

I walked into the kitchen just in time for dinner. Papá was cooking up his favorite dish, paella with chicken, sausage, rice, vegetables, and seafood. Dee-lish!

"*Huele delicioso*, Papá."

He smiled. "Glad it smells good, Muddy-gal."

Mamá sat at the kitchen table, reading a magazine. "How was the pond, *Hija*?"

"*¡Excelente!* We found insects everywhere. *Señor* Bill was there and helped us figure out what was what." I went over to Mamá and gave her a quick hug. "We found giant water bugs, lace bugs, tons of crickets, and this cool bug called an assassin bug." Pretending to know karate, I cut my arm through the air and kicked my foot toward her. "Hiyah!"

She laughed—that is until she saw the bottom of my shoe.

"Muddy Madeleine!" she exclaimed. "Look at your feet! Look at my floor!"

My tennis shoes were covered in mud, and I had left a trail of muck all over the kitchen and hallway floors.

"Oops! *Lo siento*, Mamá. *Yo lo limpio.*" I quickly took off my shoes, opened the back door and tossed them outside.

Mamá handed me a towel and spray bottle of cleaner. "You bet you'll clean it up. Here you go, MUD-dy. Get to work."

I could tell she wasn't too mad because she had half a smile on her face.

While cleaning the floor I told my folks that Ava, on her quest to find the perfect *bicho* for her poem, chased a water bug right into the pond. They laughed as I told the tale of how it took three of us to drag her out of the mud.

"It was like she was caught in quicksand. We had to form a human chain to get her out."

"Sounds like an adventure," said Papá.

"Sure was. And if you think I'm dirty, then you should see her. Her mom's gonna kill her when she comes home without her shoes."

"*¿Qué pasó con sus zapatos?*" asked Mamá.

"Stuck in the mud," I said, from under the table, cleaning up my mess. "We searched and searched, but couldn't find 'em." I chuckled. "Guess they belong to *Señor* Bill now."

"Dinner's ready," announced Papá.

Perfect timing. I wiped away the last track of my size-five shoe and joined the folks at the kitchen table.

After dinner, Mamá suggested I finish up my homework so I would have the rest of my weekend free.

Before shuffling off to my room, I went to the window to check on Hilandera. The sky was going dark, but there was just enough light for me to see her on the web. She looked like a shadow hanging in midair. With the lack of light, both the web and her beautiful markings were completely invisible. Since I didn't see any dangling shadows of cocooned insects nearby, I figured she'd have to endure another night munching on her web. I tapped on the window. "*Buenas noches*, Hilandera."

* * *

I threw my book bag on my bed and flopped down beside it. Murphy followed my lead, plopping himself right on top of my stuff.

"C'mon, Murphy." I sighed and, with a powerful push, rolled him over, off the bag and onto his back. All four of his legs stuck up in the air, begging for me to scratch his belly. Knowing I had no other choice, I complied.

"Okay, boy," I said, giving him one final scratch. "Time for you to go. *Bájate.*"

He looked at me, his eyes pleading for more.

"Nope. Get off." With a little extra help from me, Murphy jumped down and crawled under the bed. Being 160 pounds, only the front half of his body could fit under the bedframe. "*Perro loco,*" I giggled. What a crazy dog. His tail wagged as if he knew I was talking about him. "Time to get to work," I told him.

Just because I love to learn doesn't mean I enjoy homework. Some homework can be a real drag, but I looked forward to this particular assignment. Hilandera and creative writing? That's a great combo! Not as much fun as saving Ava from a muddy doom, but definitely a nice way to spend an evening. I pulled out my assignment and read the directions.

Poetry Assignment: An Insect for Me

¡Hola class!* This assignment combines two subjects, writing and science. Follow the directions below and you'll be on your way to becoming the next William Shakespeare and Marie Curie. Write a poem (can rhyme, but not required) about an insect. The poem must contain at least three observations you have made of an insect and/or facts you have researched. Include a picture (drawn or photographed) and the insect's common name.

<u>Due: Monday</u>

Example: A Monarch Butterfly   By: Ms. Villegas

> With wings orange, black and white
> One flower to the next, takes flight
> In search of a Milkweed in her sight
> The scarcity of this plant is a fright
>
> This plant, the only host
> No other can ever boast
> Upon which Monarch's eggs can post
> Without, her species becomes a ghost
>
> Along her migration route
> The Monarch looks around about
> With luck, a Milkweed plant has turned out
> She knows what's to be done, without a doubt
>
> Upon the leaves, her eggs she lay
> After which she flies away
> Time for her to wallow and play
> Generations live another day

<u>Hints</u>: Go outside and search for an insect. Write down your observations. What does it looks like? Where did you find it? What is it doing? How does it make you feel? What questions do you have? What does it resemble? Don't forget to have fun, too!

"Cool poem, Ms. V," I said to myself. Feeling inspired, I pulled my journal from my book bag. Reviewing my notes and drawings of Hilandera, I felt glad we had made so many entries. There was a ton of info to work with—colors, shapes and behaviors. This should be pretty easy. Well, at least the research part.

I scribbled down words and then pieced them together like a puzzle, turning them into phrases. Some rhymed. Some didn't. Some were good and some were just plain awful. In a short time, I had accumulated *muchas* sheets of paper filled with *muy* bad ideas. Those I wadded up and threw on the floor. Murphy's rear-end looked like it was covered with paper snowballs. But I'm not one who gives up easily. I kept scribbling and an hour later I had something I liked. No, I loved it. Definitely A material!

* * *

I woke up at my usual time for a Saturday, and moseyed into the kitchen for some breakfast. Throwing a waffle into the toaster, I pulled together all the necessary condiments to make a perfect Saturday morning meal—honey, strawberries and a few chocolate chips to sweeten the pot. I tossed a couple pieces of bacon into the microwave, too. After assembling all the ingredients, creating a culinary creature with chocolate eyes, strawberry lips and bacon legs, I sat at the kitchen table to devour my art. Dee-lish!

Looking out the window, I saw Mamá and Papá already busy in the vegetable garden. Murphy, who couldn't scale the tall fence around the garden, kept himself busy trying to climb his way up a Post Oak to catch a squirrel.

"*¡Buenos días,* Hilandera*!*" I said, turning my gaze toward her web.

"*¡NO ES POSIBLE!*" I jumped off my chair and ran around the table to get a better look.

She was gone.

Chapter Fifteen
Nothin' a Little Zucchini Wouldn't Fix

Panic-mode commenced. I frantically scanned the area around her web, but saw no signs of Hilandera. With my pulse racing, I couldn't focus and my eyes wandered aimlessly around the web. She usually sat right in the middle of the zigzaggin' zipper. Where could she be?

Hilandera had become more than a science project to me—she was my pet. While she was a different kind of companion than Murphy, I cared for her all the same. I couldn't throw her a ball or cuddle with her on the couch, but I enjoyed watching her build her web and worried about her finding food. If that's not a pet, then I don't know what is.

"Okay, girl," I said to myself. "Focus!"

Closing my eyes, I took a deep breath and started again.

I began my investigation of the web, which was perfectly constructed—no holes or dangling threads. Actually, the web looked brand-spankin' new. The silk

lines were taut and the
angles crisp, without any
sags. The stabilmentum
had perfect zigs to go
along with its zags. The
only thing wrong with

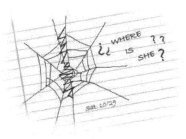

the web was its missing spider—my spider. My eyes
moved to the eaves of the porch, where the top of
her web was anchored. No Hilandera. Circling the
web, I focused my attention on its other five anchors
and, like the others, no Hilandera.

Maybe she went out for a little stroll, I thought.
But she's never done that before, at least not that I
had seen.

I shuffled back to the table to finish my breakfast,
but the cold remains of my waffle creature no longer
appealed to me. Sitting there, with my chin cradled
in my hands, I stared at the empty web. My tongue
slipped into thinking mode, right between my lips.

So absorbed by Hilandera's absence, I didn't
notice Mamá had entered the kitchen until she said,
"¡Buenos días, Hija!"

"¡Hijole!" I exclaimed, jumping out of my trance.
People have got to quit scaring me in my own
kitchen!

She laughed at the startled expression on my

face. "You look lost in thought, *Hija*. *¿Qué tienes?*"

"*No encuentro* Hilandera." I said, sulking. "That's what's wrong."

"You can't find her?" she asked, walking over to the window to take a look.

"Nope."

"How strange. A female spider typically doesn't leave her web unless she thinks she's in danger." Mamá turned her attention back to me. "Maybe Hilandera is hiding. Did you go outside and look for her?"

"No," I said. "I thought about it, but I was scared I might step on her."

"Well, *Hija*, it's too soon to worry. Why don't you get dressed and come help us in the garden? The zucchini's ripe for picking and you won't believe how good a crop we have this late in the season."

My attitude flipped like a light switch. "Does that mean we can make zucchini bread today?"

"*Sí, Hija*. You up for it?"

"Coolio!" I dropped my plate in the sink and hurried to my room to get dressed for a day of picking and baking. Mamá's recipe for zucchini bread was the best in town and she had the ribbons to prove it. For the last two years, her *pan de calabacín* had won first prize at my school's fall festival. Since we only make it when the zucchinis are fresh, I wasn't going to miss the final harvest worrying about Hilandera—especially since I wasn't sure I even needed to worry.

* * *

Two hours later I was in the kitchen surrounded by zucchinis. Mamá wasn't kidding about the crop size. Zucchinis of all sizes were piled so high on the kitchen counter they looked like the Andes mountain range. I accidently bumped into a pile and a green avalanche fell to the floor.

Luckily, we had locked Murphy outside while we washed and sorted the vegetables. Normal dogs beg for meats like *pollo, jamón, y bistec,* but *mi perro* was anything but normal. He went *loco* over *verduras,* and if he had access to all this produce there would be nothing left but a pile of carnage. When it came to vegetables, even Mamá's dog-treat trick wouldn't work. For this reason, The Murphinator was stuck outside, watching us through the window and drooling with envy.

Working as quickly as we could, knowing we could only keep him at bay for a short time, we baked our last zucchini bread of the season. Papá helped me clean up the mess, while Mamá stowed the extra zucchini in the pantry, a safe location out

of Murphy's reach. Once everything was back in its proper place, it was time to eat. Warm zucchini bread with melted butter. Dee-lish!

All the work in the garden, followed by cooking and cleaning, left me starving. Papá turned on the radio to one of the salsa stations, and we sat at the kitchen table, listening to music and stuffing our faces *con pan de calabacín* that was *delicioso*. I was so hungry I scarfed down four pieces.

Mamá had reinstated Murphy's indoor privileges and he was busy sniffing the kitchen floor and counter tops, looking for leftover shreds of zucchini. Not finding any, he looked at us and whimpered.

Papá, who couldn't resist those puppy-dog eyes, threw him a piece of bread. He quickly snatched it up and settled under the kitchen table to enjoy his treat.

With my stomach full and the day's work behind me, my mind wandered back to Hilandera. I walked to the window and surveyed the scene, hoping to find her back where she belonged.

"Is she there, *Hija?*" asked Mamá.

I shook my head. "No Hilandera ... no nothin'. Not even a *bicho* in her web."

"*Lo siento*, Muddy-gal," said Papá. "She isn't my

favorite science project of yours, but I know she is special to you."

"Yep. She sure is. I just don't understand why she would go to the trouble of creating a new web if she wasn't going to use it."

"*No sé, Hija.* Maybe she'll come back tomorrow," suggested Mamá.

I sighed. "*Espero qué sí.*"

"It's good to hope, Muddy-gal. *No pasa nada,*" said Papá, "C'mon. Let's get your mind on something else. How about a game of *Conquian?*" He looked at Mamá. "Want to play?"

She smiled. "Absolutely."

"Me, too," I said. "I could use a good card game right now." *Conquian* was my favorite game. I tried to teach Gregory how to play, but he said it was like gin rummy, which he despised, and he refused to learn—his loss.

"Pass 'em out, Muddy-gal," said Papá handing me the deck of cards.

We spent the rest of the afternoon playing. Every once in a while I looked through the window to see if Hilandera had returned, but no deal. I started to lose hope that she would ever come back.

Chapter Sixteen

The Case of the Missing Arach-A-Doo

Sunday morning I awoke to find Hilandera's web still empty. Where could she be? I went outside and quickly looked around, trying to be careful of where I stepped, but I didn't see any sign of her. I needed some help and I knew who to call.

The gang arrived after lunch.

Standing beneath the web, Ava asked, "So what happened to your arach-a-doo, *amiga?*"

"*No sé,*" I replied.

"My brain-power doesn't come cheap," she teased. "But I'll give it to you, *amiga*, for next to nothing."

Gregory's eyes widened and his mouth gaped open to one side. "You're gonna charge her?"

Javier shifted his gaze from Gregory to Ava and then to me. I stood facing her, with my arms folded across my chest, preparing for an intense negotiation.

Ava's head cocked to one side. She looked as if she was considering his question, but I knew better. She definitely wanted something, but what I didn't know.

She walked over to Gregory and put her arm around his shoulders. "Don't you think we should at least get a cookie out of it?"

I smiled. This would be easy. "How about something better?" I suggested.

"Whatcha offering?" she asked.

Putting on my best poker face, I proposed the deal. "One slice of Mamá's famous zucchini bread ... one for each of you."

"Three slices," she countered, "and don't forget the butter."

Gregory licked his lips.

Javier had a look of disgust on his face. "I'm not eating no slimy zucchini. Gross!"

"You can't even taste the zucchini," blurted Gregory.

"No way!" said Javier, shaking his head.

Pretending to intimidate Ava, I narrowed my eyes and glared at her. She slapped her right hand over her mouth, trying to hold back a giggle.

"Two pieces of *pan de calabacín* for you and Gregory." I jerked my head toward Javier. "And two cookies for the Lizard King. Final offer."

Ava and Javier exchanged a grin. "Deal!" she said and we shook on it.

Gregory clapped his hands together. "Let's eat!"

"Not yet, pal," I replied. "You gotta earn it. Let's find Hilandera."

Gregory looked a bit disappointed, but I knew he'd snap out of it. He always thinks first with his stomach, but then his brain quickly kicks into gear.

Javier was the first to jump in with a suggestion. "Could she have been eaten by a bird?"

We all looked at the web. "It looks in pretty good shape," observed Gregory. "If a bird had gotten her, wouldn't the web have been destroyed?"

"Yeah," said Ava. "That bird would've swooped down faster than my mom running with my little brother to the bathroom before he poops himself."

"*¡Cochina!*" shouted Javier. "That's so gross, Ava."

"What can I say?" she giggled. "He's a three-year old poop monster. I don't know what Mom's feeding him, but she better get him potty trained soon 'cuz it's getting' *muy cochino* at my house."

I laughed. "Okay, enough about your brother. Let's get back to the bird theory."

"Like I was saying," continued Ava, "a bird would've ripped that web to shreds when it grabbed the arach-a-doo."

"Ava's right," agreed Gregory. "There's no way she was eaten by a bird. The web's in too good of shape."

I nodded, feeling relieved she wasn't eaten. "Okay, what else could've happened?"

"Maybe she froze to death," suggested Javier. "Our *clima* lately has been *muy frío.*"

"There's an idea!" I said. "Anyone know how cold it got on Friday night?"

"Not a clue," announced Ava.

Gregory shook his head. "Me neither."

"I'll go find out. Wait here," I said and ran inside.

Mamá and Papá were working on a puzzle in the family room, with Murphy sleeping at their feet. So as not to wake him, I whispered to Mamá, "*¿Puedo usar su celular, por favor?*"

132

"Why do you need my cell phone, *Hija?*" asked Mamá, placing a corner piece into the puzzle. "It's still charging."

"We're trying to figure out what happened to Hilandera and I wanna look up some stuff," I explained.

"Here, Muddy-gal," said Papá, handing me his phone. "Use mine."

"*¡Gracias!*" I gave him a quick peck on the cheek and bolted out the door. Murphy, who was still asleep, never knew I was there.

I had only been gone for a minute, but that was plenty of time for the gang to get distracted. They had found Murphy's soccer ball and were busy kicking it around.

"Got the phone," I announced, holding it up for them to see.

Ava trapped the ball with her foot and then kicked it to Gregory. "Cool, *amiga*. Didya find out how long it takes to make an arach-a-doo Popsicle?"

"Dunno yet," I said, pulling up the Web.

They continued to kick around the ball while I typed 'What temperature kills a garden spider.' While the phone searched for websites, I watched Javier lob the soccer ball to Gregory, who headed it to Ava.

She took control of the ball and charged toward Gregory. Ava used the classic *Maradana* move, spinning around him so fast he couldn't find his way back to the make-shift goal. Taking Javier totally by surprise, she scored a goal between two trees without even breaking a sweat. Her footwork rocks, I thought.

"And she scores!" shouted Ava, thrusting her fists into the air.

I smiled and looked back at the phone. I clicked on a site, scanned it and then went to another. Ms. Villegas regularly drilled us to not believe everything we read on the internet, lecturing the importance of multiple sources. Obviously her lectures had sunk in.

In the meantime, Ava had scored two more goals, one on each boy, so they changed their strategies and teamed up against her.

"Now it's even," laughed Ava. "Bring it on, *amigos*."

"Game over, guys," I said. "I found something."

Chapter Seventeen

Fast Cars, Buttons and Yellow Pieces of Fuzz

Gregory picked up the ball and the three of them ran over, huddling around me under Hilandera's web.

"Whatcha got, Muddy?" asked Gregory.

"I was hopin' to find a specific temp, but nothing came up. All the sites pretty much said the same thing. Evidently, it needs to be really cold for a long time for spiders to die."

"That's useless," said Javier.

"I thought so, too, at first," I said, "but then I looked up Friday night's weather. It was a high of 48°F with a low of 39°F—"

"She couldn't've frozen," interjected Gregory. "'Cuz it doesn't freeze 'til 32."

"Yep." I nodded.

"Okay," said Ava. "So if the arach-a-doo didn't become a Popsicle, then what else could've happened?"

"Maybe she was just old," suggested Javier. "She could've keeled over and fell off the web."

I sighed. *"Posible."*

"Have you looked on the ground yet?" asked Gregory.

"Not really," I replied.

Ava patted me on the back. "Well, let's start there, *amiga.*"

We spread out, crawling around the area on our

hands and knees, and combed through the blades of grass with our fingers. I came across my long lost Matchbox car, but no Hilandera.

"Anybody find anything?" I hollered.

"I found a purple button," announced Ava.

"Toss it here, girl," I said. "That's from my coat." She threw it to me and I put it in my pocket.

"I think this used to be a tennis ball," said Gregory holding up a quarter-sized piece of yellow fuzz sticking to a piece of rubber.

"That would be Murphy's." I laughed. "Tennis balls don't last long around him."

"I got some ants over here," said Javier, who was directly beneath the web.

While this search was productive—having found the missing button from my coat and my favorite race car with the yellow flames on the hood—it was not helpful in solving the mystery of my missing arachnid.

That's when I started thinking about Javier's ants. If she had died and fallen off of her web, then the ants living below the web could have eaten her. I stopped looking for Hilandera and sat cross-legged on the ground. Waving my arm, I hollered, "Hey, y'all. C'mon back together." The gang crawled over and sat beside me, and I told them my ant theory.

"Yeah," agreed Gregory. "I once saw some ants in my yard gobble up a dead dragonfly. It was gone in seconds."

"Awesome," said Ava, her eyes widening at the possibility of hearing a gory story. "What about the exoskeleton? Did they eat that, too?"

"Oh, yeah," said Gregory. "They got everything."

Ava grinned. "Wish I could've seen that."

"Can we get back to Hilandera, *por favor*?" I pleaded.

Javier brought us back on track. "If she fell dead to the ground, then there'd be nothing left of her to find."

Gregory shook his head. "Nope. Not a chance."

I stared at my shoelaces, racking my brain for another idea. Finally, after who knows how long, I came up with one. "*¡Esperen!* Wait a minute, guys!"

Looking up from my shoes, I saw all my friends sitting there with their tongues sticking out. They were laughing.

"I can't believe you're making fun of me right now!" I said, somewhat kidding, but not really. "This is serious!"

That made them laugh even harder.

"It's just a spider, Muddy," suggested Javier.

"How would you feel if I said that about Ted and Fred?" I asked, feeling ticked off. "Wouldn't you care if they, all of sudden, went missing?"

"That's different," said Javier. "They're my pets—"

"HILANDERA IS MY PET, TOO!"

All three of them stared at me, no longer smiling.

I took a deep breath and let it out slowly, telling myself to chill as I exhaled. *"Lo siento, amigos.* I shouldn't have yelled."

"We were just teasin', Muddy," said Gregory, apprehensively.

I nodded. "I know, pal." Turning my attention to Javier, I said, "And you're kinda right, Javier. Hilandera is not like Ted, Fred or even Murphy, but she's ... well ... special."

"'Nuf said, *amiga*," smiled Ava. "We're sorry, too."

With a smile, Javier held out his fist toward me and we exchanged a bump. "We cool?" he asked.

I winked. "Course we are."

"Alright, alright, alright," said Ava. "Let's move on from this touchy-feely stuff and get back to business."

"Now, what was your idea, Muddy?" asked Gregory.

"Where was I?"

"All we heard was '*¡Esperen!*'" said Javier, with a dramatic flair that resembled my own. "And we're still waiting."

"*¿Esperen?* ... *¿Esperen?* ... Oh, yeah!*" I remembered and snapped my fingers together. "Maybe she didn't die. Maybe she moved her web somewhere else."

"Why would she do that, *amiga*?" asked Ava.

"That wind storm the other night was pretty *loco*. What if she thought it was too *peligroso*?" I suggested.

"But if it was too dangerous why did she rebuild her web in the same place?" argued Javier, pointing to the intact web. "Why would she go to all that trouble if she was gonna move the next day?"

"I know!" said Ava, staring at the web. "I think it's 'cuz she didn't have any food." She turned her attention to me. "How long has she been missin', *amiga*?"

"Since Friday."

"So it's been two days and look at the web. It's empty!"

"No, duh," teased Javier. "Remember? That's why we're here—to look for the spider."

Ava's lips curled up in annoyance. "I'm not talkin' about the spider, Lizard King. Check it out. No bugs."

She was right! I jumped to my feet. "That totally makes sense. I'm sure she's got another web around here somewhere."

"Alright, peeps," commanded Ava. "Let's find us a web."

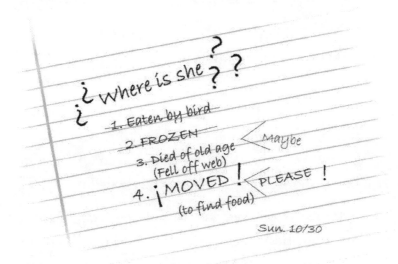

¿ where is she ? ? ?
1. Eaten by bird
2. FROZEN
3. Died of old age ← Maybe
   (fell off web)
4. ¡ MOVED ! ← PLEASE !
   (to find food)

Sun. 10/30

We split into two groups. Javier and Ava headed to my old swing set at the back of the yard while Gregory and I stayed near the house. He and I looked up and down the bricks, in and out of the screened porch, and under and over the patio furniture. Gregory even hoisted me into a tree so I could explore the branches for web-signs. *¡Nada!*

"Why don't we check there?" suggested Gregory, pointing to the vegetable garden. "Maybe Hilandera moved closer to the food."

I grinned. There he goes, thinking about food again. "Awesome idea, pal. With all that pollination going on, I bet there are a lot of *bichos* near those plants."

He shook his head and snickered. "You're such a dork."

"Ha! ... Ha! ... Ha!" I said and slugged him in the arm.

On our way to the garden, I looked toward the swing set to see how Ava and Javier were doing. Ava poked her head inside the clubhouse, while Javier climbed up the ladder, examining each rung on his ascent.

"Find anything, yet?" I yelled.

"Nope!" they hollered in unison.

"Jinx, Lizard King," exclaimed Ava. "You owe me a Coke."

"Aghh," he growled and kept on climbing.

Gregory and I looked at each other and laughed.

When we arrived at the fenced-in garden, I offered to look on the outside of the fence if he wanted the inside.

"Cool with me," said Gregory, opening the gate.

As I searched the perimeter of the garden, I found a few ladybugs crawling on the grapevines anchored to the fence and almost stepped in a fire ant mound nestled against one of the posts. Barely grazing the mound with my foot, the ants swarmed the area, and I quickly leapt out of their way. After escaping the angry ants, I came across the remains of an old web, torn and tattered, clinging to a corner of the fence. The web could have been hers, but I didn't have any evidence for or against that possibility, so I stayed hopeful.

"I got nothin' here, Gregory. How 'bout you?"

"Nope," he said, tiptoeing over the zucchini and squash plants, careful not to step on the outstretched vines. "I looked in all the containers and didn't see any spiders or webs."

I sighed and turned my head toward the swing set. "Maybe they found something."

From the looks of it, Ava and Javier had given up their search. They were flying through the air, riding my old swings. I heard Ava tease Javier.

"C'mon, Lizard King," she yelled. "Can't ya go any higher?"

"THREE ... TWO ... ONE ... JUMP!" yelled Javier, and the two leapt from their individual swings into a pile of leaves.

Gregory and I ran down the hill to join them. What started out as a simple roll in the leaves turned into a colossal leaf fight. Someone, whose identity remains unknown, shoved a fistful of leaves down the back of my shirt. While I dealt with those, Gregory snuck up behind me and smashed ground-up leaves into my hair. I was just about to get him back with a handful of leaves to his face when I heard someone call my name.

"Muddy-gal."

"Hold up, *amigos*," I shouted, putting my hands together in the shape of a T. "Time out."

"No way, Muddy," kidded Javier, coming toward me with a fistful of dried oak leaves. "You're mine."

I saw my dad standing on the back porch.

"Muddy-gal," he yelled.

"Seriously ... stop!" I said.

Javier froze, with his hands above his head.

"*¿Sí, Papá?*"

"*Necesito mi celular.*"

"Comin'," I replied, pulling his phone out of my pocket.

Javier huffed in defeat and dropped the leaves. He, along with Ava and Gregory, followed me up the hill.

"Here ya go," I said to Papá, giving him the phone.

"*¡Gracias! ¿Gustas una rebanada de calabacín?*" he asked.

Javier groaned. Ava and Gregory looked at me, their eyes pleading for a translation.

I laughed. "Would you like a slice of zucchini bread?"

"You bet," said Gregory, spitting a piece of leaf out of his mouth. "*Dos, por favor.*"

"Get the rest of those leaves out of your hair," smiled Papá, "and then c'mon in."

Ava bent over and combed her long blond hair

with her fingers. A bunch of leaves fell to the ground. I pulled a few remaining pieces from the back of her head, and she did the same for me. Javier and Gregory took care of themselves. After a few more shakes, we went inside.

Papá took the bread from the oven, while I grabbed the butter and some cookies for Javier. A deal's a deal.

All of us, except Papá, plopped down at the kitchen table and devoured our snack.

"Gotta make a call, Muddy-gal," he said. "*¿Estás bien?*"

"*Sí*, Papá. We're good."

"*Gracias, Señor* Morales," said Javier.

"Yeah, thanks Mr. M," agreed Ava.

"Whank wou," muffled Gregory with a mouthfull of bread.

"*De nada, niños,*" said Papá as he walked out of the kitchen.

I swallowed a big chunk of buttery *pan*. "Did y'all see any signs of Hilandera down by the swing set?"

Ava frowned. "Sorry, *amiga*. We found a lot of webs—"

148

"But none of them had zigzaggin' zippers," concluded Javier.

Gregory stuffed another hunk of bread in his mouth. "I iddent ew'n 'ind a wobweb."

"*¿Tienes otras ideas?*" I asked.

"No more ideas here," said Ava, tapping her noggin.

"*Nada,*" agreed Javier.

Gregory swallowed. "Zilch."

My hopes were dashed. I laid my head down onto my folded arms resting on the table. "I guess I'll never know what happened to her."

Ava hopped off her chair and walked over to me. With her hips, she pushed me halfway off the chair and sat beside me. "C'mon, *amiga.* Let's go kick the boys' butts in soccer—that'll make ya feel better."

I didn't respond.

"Oh, no! Did you just ignore me?" she snarked, pushing me further off the chair.

I tried to push back, but Ava had more momentum and I crumbled to the floor. She laughed and held her hand out for me to grab, which I did. But now it was my turn, and I pulled her to the linoleum.

Ava hit the floor with a thud, and we burst out laughing.

149

"No one's kickin' our butts," defied Gregory, returning Ava's soccer challenge.

"Yeah, it's on," said Javier, giving Gregory a pre-celebratory fist bump.

Murphy, who had just woken up from his afternoon nap, strolled into the kitchen. Gregory and Javier, who were too busy planning our defeat, didn't see him come into the room.

Ava and I exchanged a look—we were thinking the same thing. Slowly, we stood up, and I sidestepped my way to the back door. Carefully turning the knob, I eased the door open. After giving Ava a nod, we sprang into action.

"Last one out gets slimed by The Murphinator!" I yelled, and Ava and I took off, slamming the door behind us.

We heard the muffled cries of the trapped boys being clobbered by Murphy.

Chapter Eighteen
I Vant to Suck Your Guts

That night I sat on the living room couch by the window, trying to read a book, feeling totally distracted. Ava had been right about one thing. The soccer game did take my mind off Hilandera—at least for a little while—but she was dead wrong when she said we would beat the boys. After our dirty trick, they were determined to get even. Covered in dog slobber, they beat us 7-5. Oh well, maybe next time.

Mamá sat beside me on the couch knitting a scarf. She hoped to have it done for me before winter, but, by the looks of it, I wouldn't get it 'til next year.

"*¿Qué pasa, Hija?*" she asked. "You haven't turned a page in ten minutes."

"Yeah," I muttered. "Kinda having trouble stayin' focused."

She laid her knitting beside her on the couch. "Hilandera?"

"*Sí*. ... I thought we would find her today and it's frustrating not knowing what happened to her."

Mamá nodded. "You really grew to care for her."

I sighed. "I know spiders like her don't live that long—"

"About a year. Sometimes more," said Mamá.

"Yeah, but I was hoping I'd have more time with her than I got. Just wish I could've, at least, seen her eat something." I let out a deep sigh. "Did you know she had a sucking stomach? That would've been so awesome to see her suck up a fly, just like your old spider, Charlotte."

Mamá smiled and then made a loud slurping noise with her tongue.

"*¿Qué fue eso?*" I laughed.

"That was me sucking you up like a fly." She jumped into a squat on the couch, leaned toward me and tickled my sides. "SCHLURPPPP."

Fighting back, I tried to get to the weak spot under her arms. Mamá had started an all-out tickle war and I wasn't going to let her win. I kicked my legs and her knitting fell to the floor. Just as I was about to go in for the kill—using the famous 'Here Comes Mister Finger' move—I saw her.

"Stop! Stop! Stop!" I yelled. "There she is!" I sat up on my knees so quickly that Mamá fell off the couch, rear-end first, right onto her knitting needles.

"Youch!"

"You okay?" I asked, reaching my hand out to help her.

Mamá took my hand and pulled herself off the floor. Rubbing her rear-end, she laughed. "*Sí*. Luckily the tips weren't sticking up. What happened? Who'd you see?"

"Hilandera!"

"Noooo?" She quickly knelt beside me on the couch and looked out the window.

There was Hilandera, sitting in the middle of her new web. Even though this web was just a few feet from the old one, her new location was quite different. Instead of building it over a gusty wind tunnel, like before, this time she wove her web in front of the outdoor flood light.

"I can't believe Gregory and I didn't see her today." I pointed to the web. "We looked right there."

"Maybe she was in transition, *Hija*. Who knows?"

153

"Yeah, I'm just glad she's back!" I leapt to my feet and jumped on the couch. Between each leap, I shouted "THIS ... IS ... SO ... COOLIO!"

I flopped back on the couch, thinking if it weren't for Mamá's tickle fight, I never would've seen Hilandera. I probably owed Papá his fair share of the credit, too. Before leaving the house for his after-dinner run, Papá had turned on the backyard lights and let Murphy outside to play. Without the light, she would have been invisible.

Murphy, who was still outside, jumped close to the window, trying to catch a moth flying up to the light. I started to think aloud, "Moths ... light ... Hilandera."

"*¡Qué padre!* That's it!" I said, with a snap of my fingers.

"*¿Qué?*"

"She needed the light, Mamá! ... To attract the *bichos* to her web."

"*Qué inteligente,*" she said.

I smiled. "Me or *la araña?*"

"Both!" She laughed and tousled my hair with her fingers.

"Stop it, Mamá," I said, giving her a wink. "You'll mess up my doo."

154

Turning my attention back to Hilandera, I was thrilled to see her web surrounded by buzzing *bichos*. Beetles, moths and gnats swarmed all around her.

"Let's go outside and get some pictures," suggested Mamá.

"Coolio!" I jumped off the couch. "I'll get the camera—"

"And I'll get the step ladder so—"

"We can get up close and personal!"

"Meet you *afuera*," she said and rushed off to get the ladder.

I grabbed the camera from the closet and met her outside, underneath the light.

We set up the ladder and camera just in time to see Hilandera catch her first prey, a moth. As soon as the moth hit the web, Hilandera, as quick as my camera's flash, dashed over to it. At first I didn't see any silk—only the moth spinning between her back two pairs of legs. Then, as if by magic, the moth vanished and all that was left was a cocoon.

I snapped pictures throughout the entire process. The camera was set to sports mode with fast clicks, so I got lots of shots. CLICK ... CLICK ... CLICK ... CLICK ... CLICK ... CLICK ... CLICK ... CLICK.

After encasing the moth in silk, I thought Hilandera would start sucking it up, but she didn't. Like a ballerina, she gracefully moved to the upper right-hand corner of the web and stayed there— quiet and still.

"*¿Qué pasa?*" I lowered my camera and turned to Mamá. "What's she waiting for?"

"That!" Mamá pointed at the web, where I saw a beetle struggling to get free.

Once again, Hilandera sprang into action, as did I with my camera. This time, she was more like a bull than a dancer as she brutally wrapped the *bicho* over and over again with her silk.

CLICK ... CLICK ... CLICK.

While she finished cocooning the beetle, another moth had trapped itself in her web. She noticed the moth almost immediately and sprinted across the web to where it had landed. As with the others, Hilandera quickly wrapped this new prey in silk.

CLICK. I took a final picture—Hilandera surrounded by a three-course meal.

She returned to her first victim. With her head pointed to the ground, she used her front left leg and one of her middle right legs to bring the silk-encased moth to her head. She gave the moth the kiss of death and, with that, 'Countess Hilandera' sucked away its life.

Chapter Nineteen
One More Paper Snowball

BUZZ! ... BUZZ! ... BUZZ!

I had set my alarm to wake me up early the next morning so I could spend some time with Hilandera before school. Plus, today was Halloween and I needed extra time getting dressed—pinning all those chimpanzees to my clothes was not something I wanted to do with haste. No pricked fingers for me!

Sitting on the couch, with a dozen stuffed chimpanzees stuck to my shirt, I flipped through the pictures on the camera. I had some incredible shots of Hilandera and her three victims. These will be great to use for my poetry assignment, I thought.

Papá, still in his pajamas, walked over to the couch and sat beside me. "I heard you had a nice night of picture taking, Muddy-gal. May I take a look?" He pointed to the camera.

I turned the camera so he and I could both see the images, and I flipped to my favorite one.

"*¡Muy bien!*" he said. "Maybe you'll be a *fotógrafa* when you grow up."

"But I want to be a writer," I said. "How about a photo journalist instead?"

"Even better," he said. "*¿Cómo se dice eso en español?*"

"Ohh, c'mon, Papá," I groaned. "It's too early for a language lesson."

He gave me a look that said, 'No, it's not.'

"Okay. ¿Ehhh ... *foto* ... *perio* ... *foto-periodista?*"

"*Muy bien*, Muddy-gal." He patted me on the back.

I laughed. "Could you help me print out this picture so I can include it with my writing assignment today? *¿Por favor,* Papá?"

"You bet." He took the camera and headed to his office.

I turned my attention to Hilandera. Her web still had some leftovers stuck to it, but all the damage caused by the moths and beetle had been fixed—no more holes. This gave me an idea. I reached over to my book bag, lying next to me on the couch, and took out my homework. Looking at the clock on the mantle, I saw it was still early. I had time to make some repairs of my own, and pulled out my poem along with a few sheets of blank paper from my bag. After crossing out two lines, I added a couple more and then scribbled out a few words, replacing them with others.

"Oh, yeah," I said to myself. "That'll do." I transferred the changes to a clean piece of paper and crumpled up the old one.

Murphy strolled up to the couch just in time to get hit in the head by another paper snowball.

I laughed and gave his ears a good scratch. "*Lo siento*, Murphy. You just keep getting in the way of all my rejects."

He sniffed one of my chimpanzees. With lightning speed, he clamped his jaw on the stuffed animal and tugged.

"No, you don't," I said. "Give me that." I pulled the stuffed chimp out of his mouth, amazed at how quickly he was able to douse it with his slobber.

He went for another. "Leave it!" I yelled, cupping the targeted chimp in my hands. For once, he listened to me and lay on the floor.

Just as I finished wiping the slobber off the chimp and onto my pants, Papá returned from the study, holding the picture. Mamá followed him into the room with a mug in each hand filled with her

'nectar of life.' He handed me the photo and sat on the floor in front of the couch, next to Murphy.

"*¡Gracias*, Papá!*"

"*De nada*, Muddy-gal."

Murphy rolled over and Papá scratched his belly.

Mamá handed Papá one of the coffee mugs and then sat next to me on the couch. "Is that your assignment, *Hija*?

"*Sí*. Wanna hear it?"

"*¡Definitivamente!*" said Mamá.

"*¡Claro qué sí!*" agreed Papá. "Read us your latest masterpiece."

I began, "'An Ode to Hilandera,' by Madeleine Morales." Looking up from the paper, I saw they were smiling, cleared my throat and continued.

Long lanky legs
Tapping on a web
Waiting in the middle
Moving her legs like a fiddle
She works to catch her dinner
So she doesn't get thinner
Fixing the holes quietly
She sneaks up on her prey silently
Hilandera needs to be fed
That's why she sits on her web

163

"The End," I said.

Mamá set her coffee mug on the end table and clapped. "¡*Muy bien, Hija!*"

"Bravo!" shouted Papá, startling Murphy, who jumped to his feet and barked.

"RAWF! ... RAWF!"

Smiling, I turned my attention to Hilandera and said, "Welcome to your new home, gal. Thanks for stickin' around." I snorted. Sometimes I just crack myself up!

Spanish Glossary

A mi me gusta la miel también (ah mee meh goos-TAH lah mee-EL tam-bee-EN) I love honey, too

Adiós (ah-dee-OS) Goodbye

Afuera (Ah-foo-EH-rah) Outside

Aguacates (AH-wah-CAH-tehs) Avocados

¡Ahí está! (ah-EE es-TAH) There she is!

Ahora (ah-OH-rah) Now

Amiga/o/os (ah-MEE-gah/ ah-MEE-goh/ah-MEE-gohs) Friend (female)/ Friend (male)/ Friends

Araña (ah-RAH-nyah) Spider

Asi es (ah-SEE es) That's correct

!Ay¡ (i) Oh!

¿Ayudarte con qué? (ah-yoo-DAR-teh cohn keh) Help with what?

Bájate (BAH-hah-teh) You get off

Bella (BEH-lyah) Beautiful

Bicho/Bichos (BEE-choh/BEE-chohs) Insect/Insects

Bistec (bees-TEHK) Steak

Blanco (BLAHN-coh) White

Buenas noches (boo-eh-nahs NOH-chehs) Good night

Buenos días (boo-eh-nohs DEE-ahs) Good morning

Claro que sí (CLAH-roh keh see) Of course; by all means

Clima (CLEE-mah) Climate; weather

Cochina/o (coh-CHEE-nah/noh) Gross or nasty

Comen bichos (coh-MEN BEE-chohs) They eat insects

¿Cómo se dice eso en español? (COH-moh seh dee-seh EH-soh en es-pah-NYOLE) How do you say that in Spanish?

Computadora (cohm-poo-tah-DOR-rah) Computer

Con (cohn) With

Conquian (cohn-KEE-ahn) A Mexican card game similar to gin rummy

De nada (deh nah-dah) You're welcome

¡Definitivamente! (deh-fee-nee-tee-vah-MEN-teh) Definitely!

Delicioso (deh-lee-see-OH-soh) Delicious

Dónde está (dohn-deh es-TAH) Where is

¿Dónde está tu araña? (dohn-deh es-TAH too ah-RAH-nyah) Where is your spider?

Dos por favor (dohs por fah-VOR) Two please

La capitana (lah cah-pee-TAH-nah) The captain (female)

Elegante (eh-leh-GAHN-teh) Elegant

Ella no es peligrosa (EH-yah noh es peh-lee-GROH-sah) She is not dangerous

¿Eres tu? (EH-rehs too) Is that you?

¡Esa es! (EH-sah es) That's her!

¡Esperen! (es-PEH-rehn) To expect, wait or hope

Espero qué sí (es peh-ROH keh see) I hope so

Está bien conmigo (Es-TAH bee-en cohn-mee-goh) It's okay; good with me

¿Estás bien? (es-TAHS bee-en) Are you good? Are you okay?

¡Exacto! (ex-SAHC-toh) Exact

¡Excelente! (ex-seh-LEN-teh) Excellent!

Fotógrafa (foh-TOH-grah-fah) Photographer (female)

Foto-periodista (FOH-toh-peh-ree-oh-DEES-tah) Photo journalist (female)

Frío (FREE-oh) Cold temperature

¡Gracias! (GRAH-see-ahs) Thank you!

¿Gustas una rebanada de calabacín? (goos-TAHS OO-nah reh-bah-NAH-dah deh cahl-lah-bah-SEEN) Would you like a slice of zucchini bread?

Hija (EE-hah) Daughter

¡Hijole! (ee-HO-lay) An expression of surprise similar to yikes or wow

Hilandera (ee-lahn-DEH-rah) The spider's name; literal translation, woman who spins

¡Hola! (oh-lah) Hello!

Huele delicioso (oo-EH-leh deh-lee-see-OH-soh) Smells delicious

Interesante (in-teh-reh-SAHN-teh) Interesting

Jamón (hah-MOHN) Ham

Javier (HAH-vee-ehr) Pronunciation for Javier's name

Listo (LEES-toh) Ready; clever; *voila*; *presto*

Lo siento (loh SEE-EN-toh) I'm sorry

¡Lo tengo! (loh TEN-goh) I got it!

Loco (LOH-coh) Crazy

Mamá (mah-MAH) Mom

Manzana (mahn-SAHN-nah) Apple

Maradona (mah-rah-DOH-nah) The maradona is a soccer maneuver named after Argentine soccer legend Diego Maradona, in which the player dribbling the ball spins 360 degrees.

Mariella (mah-ree-el-lah) Pronunciation for Muddy Madeleine's name

Me gustan los bichos (meh goos-TAHN lohs BEE-chohs) I love insects

Mi (mee) My

Mi abuelo (mee ah-boo-eh-loh) My grandfather

Mi familia (mee fah-MEE-lee-ah) My family

Mi perro (mee PEH-rroh) My dog

Miel (mee-EL) Honey

Milagros (mee-LAH-grohs) Pronunciation for Muddy Madeleine's name

Mis estudiantes (mees es-too-dee-AHN-tehs) My students

Morales (moh-RAHL-es) Pronunciation for Muddy Madeleine's last name

Mucho/as (MOO-choh/chahs) Much

Muy (MOO-e) Very

¡Muy bien! (MOO-e bee-en) Very good!

Muy interesante (MOO-e in-teh-reh-SAHN-teh) Very interesting

Nada (nah-dah) Nothing

Necesito mi celular (neh-seh-see-TOH mee seh-loo-lahr) I need my cell phone

Niños (NEE-nyos) Children

No (noh) No

No encuentro (noh en-coo-EN-troh) I can't find

No es posible (noh es poh-SEE-bleh) Not possible

No más arañas para mi (noh mahs ah-RAH-nyahs PAH-rah mee) No more spiders for me

No pasa nada (noh PAH-sah nah-dah) Don't worry about it; you'll be fine

No sé (noh seh) I don't know

No tengas miedo (noh TEN-gahs mee-EH-doh) Don't be scared

Nopales con huevos (no-PAHL-es cohn oo-EH-vohs) Cacti with eggs

¡Oye! (oh-yeh) Hey!

Pan (pahn) Bread

Pan de calabacín (pahn deh cah-lah-bah-SEEN) Zucchini bread

Papá (pah-PAH) Dad

Peligroso (peh-lee-GROH-soh) Dangerous

Perro loco (PEH-rroh LOH-coh) Crazy dog

Pollo (POH-yoh) Chicken

Por favor (por fah-VOR) Please

¿Por qué? (por keh) Why?

¿Por qué no? (por keh noh) Why not?

Posible (poh-SEE-bleh) Possible

¡Pregunta excelente! (preh-GOON-tah ex-seh-LEN-teh) Excellent question!

Prometo (proh-MEH-toh) I promise

¿Puedo usar su celular, por favor? (Poo-eh-doh oo-SAHR soo seh-loo-lahr por fah-VOR) Can I use your cell please?

¿Qué? (keh) What?

¡Qué Dios los bendiga! (keh dee-OHS lohs ben-dee-gah) May God bless you

¡Qué dramático! (keh drah-MAH-tee-coh) How dramatic!

¿Qué es eso? (keh es EH-soh) What is that?

¿Qué fue eso? (keh foo-EH EH-soh) What was that?

Qué inteligente (keh in-teh-lee-HEN-teh) That's smart

Qué lleguen a la extinción (keh yeh-gehn ah lah ex-teen-see-OHN) May they reach extinction

¡Qué padre! (keh PAH-dreh) Wow! A feeling of excitement

¿**Qué pasa?** (keh PAH-sah) What's up?

"**Qué pasó con sus zapatos?** (keh pah-SOH cohn soos zah-PAH-tohs) What happened to her shoes?

¿**Qué te parece?** (keh teh pah-REH-seh) What do you think?

¡**Qué tengas un buen día!** (keh ten-gahs oon boo-EN DEE-ah) You have a nice day!

¿**Qué tienes?** (keh tee-en-NEHS) What's wrong? Literal translation, what do you have?

¡**Qué verguenza!** (keh vehr-goo-ehn-zah) How embarrassing!

¿**Quieres hacer esto?** (kee-eh-rrehs ah-SEHR ES-toh) Do you want to do this?

Ranas (RAH-nahs) Frogs

Rápido (RAH-pee-doh) Fast

Señor (seh-NYOR) Mister

Sí (see) Yes

Sientate (see-EN-tah-teh) You sit

También (tahm-bee-EN) Too

¿**Te acuerdas?** (teh ah-coo-ehr-DAHS) Do you remember?

¿**Te parece bien, Papá? (**teh pah-reh-SEH bee-en, pah-PAH) Does that seem okay with you, Dad?

Te prometo (teh proh-meh-TOH) I promise

Tener un gran fin de semana (teh-NERR oon grahn feen deh seh-MAH-nah) Have a great weekend

Tienen ocho (tee-ehn-NEHN Oh-choh) They have eight

Tienen seis (tee-ehn-NEHN seh-ees) They have six

¿Tienes otras ideas? (tee-ehn-es OH-trahs ee-deh-AHS) Do you have other ideas?

Trae tres para nosotros por favor (trah-EH trehs PAH-rah noh-soh-trohs por-fah-VOR) Bring three for us please

Treinta minutos (TREH-een-tah mee-NOO-tohs) Thirty minutes

Tres (trehs) Three

Tu araña (too ah-RAH-nyah) Your spider

Ven a la ventana y te presento (ven ah lah ven-TAH-nah ee teh preh-sehn-TOH) Come to the window and I'll introduce you to

Ven acá (ven ah-KAH) Come here

Verduras (ver-DOO-rahs) Vegetables

Villegas (vee-YEH-gahs) Pronunciation for Ms. Villegas

Y (e) And

Yo lo limpio (Yoh loh LEEM-pee-oh) I'll clean it up

Yo sé (Yoh seh) I know

Yo también te amo (yoh tam-bee-EN teh AH-moh) I love you, too

Science Glossary

Abdomen (AB-duh-muhn) The third section of an insect's three body parts or the second section of an arachnid's two body parts

Andes Mountains (Ahn-dees) The world's longest continental mountain range; 310 miles wide and 4,300 miles long; located in South America; runs north to south through Venezuela, Colombia, Ecuador, Peru, Bolivia, Chile, and Argentina

Antenna (an-TEN-uh) A jointed, movable part occurring in pairs on the head of an insect; used as a sensory tool, to feel things; *plural* antennae

Arachnid (uh-RAK-nid) A class of invertebrate animals that have eight legs and two body parts, such as spiders, scorpions, ticks, and mites

Argiope (ar-GUY-oh-pee) A spider, in the arachnid class, that often has a colorful abdomen; also known as black and yellow garden spiders, sipper spiders, corn spiders, and writing spiders; the scientific name for *argiope*s that use a stabilmentum in their web is *Argiope aurantia* (ar-GUY-oh-pee uh-RUHN-tia)

Bug (bug) This word is often used to describe any tiny creature with legs; bug actually refers to a group of insects that have forewings and lack teeth, such as beetles

Carnivorous (kahr-NIV-ER-uhs) Something that eats meat

Curie, Marie (kyoo-REE, muh-REE) A Polish-born, French-naturalized scientist who received Nobel Prizes in physics in 1903 and chemistry in 1911; she worked primarily in radioactivity

Einstein, Albert (ahyn-stahyn, al-bert) A German-born, American-naturalized scientist who developed the general theory of relativity

Entomologist (en-tuh-MOL-uh-JIST) Someone who studies insects

Exoskeleton (ek-so-SKEL-ih-ton) A hard external covering that protects an animal's body

Extinct (ik-STINGKT) Something that is no longer in existence

Goodall, Jane (GOOD-awl, jeyn) A British primatologist who is best known for her 45-year study of chimpanzees in Tanzania

Head (hed) The head of an insect is referred to as head; whereas, a spider's head is also known as a cephalothorax (sef-uh-loh-THAW-rax); a spider's legs are attached to the head

Hypothesis (hahy-POTH-uh-sis) An educated guess to explain the occurrence of something

Insect (in-sekt) A small animal that breathes air and has three body parts, three pairs of legs and one or two pairs of wings

Insectivore (in-SEK-tuh-VOWR) An animal that only eats insects, such as an anteater, meerkat or woodpecker

Invertebrate (in-VUR-tuh-brit) An animal that does not have a backbone or spine

Orb Weaver Spider A spider that weaves an orb-shaped (round, wheel-shaped, flat) web; spiders are classified into families by the type of web they weave; orb weaver spiders are the third largest spider family

Plausible (PLAW-zuh-buh) Appearing to be truthful, reasonable or possible

Pollen (POL-uhn) the fertilizing part of a flowering plant; pollen contains cells that help the plant reproduce

Pollination (pol-un-NEY-shuhn) The process of transferring pollen from the anthers of a flower to the stigma of another or the same flower; without this process, fertilization cannot occur

Pollinator (POL-uh-ney-tor) An animal that assists in pollination

Prey (pray) An animal that is hunted or killed for food

Mexican Jumping Beans. These beans are native to Mexico; the larva of a moth lives inside the seed pod; when the pod is heated, the larva move to avoid the heat; this movement gives the appearance of a jumping bean

Non-toxic (nont-tok-sik) Not having a poisonous effect

Seed (seed) A product of fertilization

Silk (silk) A protein fiber produced by a spider; researchers have discovered that spider silk is five times stronger than steel

Spinerette (SPIN-uh-RET) The part of a spider's body where it spins a silk thread

Stabilmentum (Stay-bil-men-tum) A zigzag design, made of silk, on a spider's web

Sucking Stomach (SUHK-ing STUHM-uhk) A pump that draws the liquid food into the spider's digestive track

Theory (THEE-uh-REE) A proposed explanation; a guess

Thorax (tho-rax) The second (middle) part of an insect's body, between the head and the abdomen; the legs and wings are joined to the thorax

Venom (VEN-uhm) A poisonous fluid typically delivered through a bite or a sting; the venom of an *Argiope* spider is typically considered to be harmless to humans; the spider's venom liquefies the prey so it can draw it into the digestive track through its sucking stomach

Vertebrate (VUR-tuh-brit) A group within the animal kingdom, in which all the members have a spine or backbone; examples of vertebrates include humans, birds, reptiles, mammals, amphibians, and fish

Wing (wing) Connected to the insect's thorax; some insects have either one or two pairs of wings

Author Bio

After seventeen years in education, Dr. Amanda Stone Norton re-invented herself and joined the literary world as a writer and editor. Originally from Louisville, KY, Amanda now lives in Fort Worth, TX. When she's not playing outdoors with her family or working on her latest writing project, Amanda volunteers as the Executive Chair of the Texas Children in Nature Network-North Texas Region, part of a global grassroots network to connect children to nature. To learn more about Amanda and her current projects, please visit her website at www.amandastonenorton.com and follow her on Facebook, Amanda Stone Norton, Writer.

Illustrator Bio

Veronica V. Jones is a professional freelance illustrator specializing in the fantasy and science fiction genres. She began her illustration career in 2000, and has since worked on a wide variety of publications and projects including games, chapter books and comic books. She enjoys using her digital paintbrush to capture flights of fantasy, illuminating the imaginations of both young and old. Veronica lives with her family in Manassas, VA. To learn more about Veronica and her current projects, please visit her website at www.vvjones.com and follow her on Facebook, Moonshines.

A Dash of Shakespeare
with a Pinch of Curie

Writing Poetry through Scientific Observation

I am observing _____

(name of natural object)

This object looks like ...

This objects feels like ...

This object of nature reminds me of ...

I already know the following about this object of nature ...

I wonder why this object of nature ...

Poetry Time

Just as Muddy used her scientific observations to write a poem, so can you! Take your notes from the previous page and create your own "Ode to a Bug-O-Vore."

ODE TO HILANDERA
By: Muddy Madeleine Morales

Long lanky legs
Tapping on a web
Waiting in the middle
Moving her legs like a fiddle
She works to catch her dinner
So she doesn't get thinner
Fixing the holes quietly
She sneaks up on her prey silently
Hilandera needs to be fed
That's why she sits on her web

Made in the USA
Lexington, KY
30 November 2014